D1478704

SWEET LULLABY

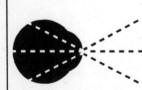

This Large Print Book carries the
Seal of Approval of N.A.V.H.

SWEET LULLABY

PAIGE WINSHIP DOOLY

THORNDIKE PRESS

A part of Gale, Cengage Learning

Detroit • New York • San Francisco • New Haven, Conn • Waterville, Maine • London

GALE
CENGAGE Learning®

LIBRARY OF CONGRESS CATALOGING-IN-PUBLICATION DATA

Dooly, Paige Winship.
    Sweet Lullaby / by Paige Winship Dooly. — Large Print edition.
      pages cm. — (Thorndike Press Large Print Christian Romance)
    ISBN-13: 978-1-4104-5762-2 (hardcover)
    ISBN-10: 1-4104-5762-1 (hardcover)
    1. Counselors—Fiction. 2. Teenage pregnancy—Fiction. 3. Single-parent families—Fiction. 4. Family secrets—Fiction. 5. Life change events—Fiction. 6. Missouri—Fiction. 7. Large type books. I. Title.
    PS3604.O575S94 2013
    813'.6—dc23
                                       2013000867

Published in 2013 by arrangement with Barbour Publishing, Inc.

Printed in Mexico
1 2 3 4 5 6 7 17 16 15 14 13

To my family — thank you so much for the support and patience you continue to show me when I'm on a deadline and can't juggle all the balls! I love you all dearly.

ONE

Josie merged into the throng of people heading down the hill toward the picnic area and allowed the masses to carry her along. The sight of the people, all rushing forward to squeeze through the small opening in the chain-link fence surrounding the church grounds, reminded her of a brief visit to New York City several years earlier. The one time she'd ventured into a subway station she'd felt like a small fish swimming in a very large school as everyone exited the subway cars shoulder to shoulder and headed for the stairs at the same time. While she didn't usually consider herself to be claustrophobic, the sensation of being trapped in the crowd encouraged her to stay above ground for the remainder of her visit. The crowds were just as big, but the fresh air somehow helped.

Growing up in the suburbs of big-city Dallas was nothing like spending time in

New York. The experience reinforced the fact that Josie — who had fallen in love with small-town life during her summers as a camp counselor — would always be a small-town girl at heart who preferred lots of open space and fewer people. She'd taken a job in Dallas when fresh out of college, but knew she'd eventually relocate to a smaller town. She'd found the perfect place when answering the ad for the live-in part-time therapist position in Lullaby, Missouri.

Josie smiled as she scanned the masses from her limited vantage point. The group drifted downhill toward the lake. It seemed Lullaby surged into a much larger population during tourist season. Her new hometown had exploded for the day. For a moment Josie was afraid she'd be crushed if she fought the masses with a sudden change of direction. No swimming upstream for this fish!

"Josie! Josie Alvarez! Over here, hon!"

Josie stood on tiptoe and tried to identify the vaguely familiar voice. Someone pressed against her back, and she resumed walking. It was impossible to locate who had called to her through the mob. Her petite stature put her at a disadvantage at a time like this. She continued to walk along until the attendees scattered into the open area across the street from the church and fanned out in search of the perfect picnic spot. The lakeside grounds formed the perfect back-drop for the event.

"Josie." This time her name was said with a hint of laughter.

Josie glanced slightly behind her and saw her new boss's grandmother hurrying to catch up. Josie smiled. "Miss Ethel, I could hear you, but I couldn't figure out where you were."

"I know. I was trying to figure out how to go in and rescue you. Would you care to join the family for lunch? We have a few blankets under that huge old hickory down by the water." She waved a hand toward the lake, and her silver bracelets sparkled in the sunlight.

"I'd love to join you." Josie sighed with relief. She hadn't wanted to eat alone, but she hadn't wanted to eat with strangers either. She'd never enjoyed this part of set-tling into a new place.

Ethel hooked Josie's left arm with her own and led her toward the water. "I tried to catch you over at the stage, but the sea of people swept you away. I hope you don't mind eating with a gaggle of young ones. I'm sure my grandchildren — at least some of them — will be joining us at some point."

"Oh, I'd love that. I miss my nieces and nephews back home."

"Where is back home?"

"Texas."

Ethel motioned toward several colorful blankets laid out in the shade of a tree.

"Someone came prepared." Josie smiled.

"I sent my grandson ahead to pick the perfect location. He did a good job, don't you think?"

"A very good job. It's wonderful." Josie shaded her eyes with her hand. A vivid blue sky formed a ceiling high above the tree's network of leaves. The late-morning sun dappled the lake's water and made it shimmer like millions of glittering diamonds. Birds dipped low as they skimmed the water and searched below the surface for their next meal. The weather was perfect — mid-80s — which was just right for a small-town picnic. "This place is a world away from where I lived before."

"Texas is a big state."

"Very." Josie agreed.

"Did you live in the city?" Ethel settled on the blanket and patted the spot beside her.

"Yes. Dallas. I did my clinical training there and fell into the perfect job. I stayed on and worked in a family therapy practice."

"Why'd you move on? You didn't like it after you'd been there awhile?"

"I loved it, but I wanted to focus on teens, and at the clinic we had to see whatever age came in. I decided I wanted to specialize and slow down a bit, get to know my clients better. I was starting to burn out."

A tiny blond skidded to a stop at the edge of the nearest blanket. "Gram! Jennie asked me to sit with her family. Can I? Please?"

"Noelle, you can't just run off like that." A frazzled pregnant teen hurried along at the little girl's heels. "I'm sorry, Gram. I stopped by the church to change from my dress into my casual clothes, and Noelle took off without me."

Ethel sent the little girl a pointed look. "You know better than to run off from your older sisters or brothers when they're caring for you, especially when we're near the lake. Do you want Brit to see you running wild? She'll make you wear your life jacket."

The little girl's eyes widened. "No."

"Then you slow down and wait for Allie next time."

"Yes, ma'am." Noelle hopped from one foot to the other. "So can I sit with Jennie?"

"May I."

Confusion marred the preschooler's features. "I guess so. She'll have to ask her

11

mom if you want to come with me."

Josie couldn't help but smile. She exchanged an amused glance with Ethel and Allie.

"I wasn't asking to go with you, Noelle. I was correcting the way you asked. The proper way to phrase it is 'May I sit with Jennie?' "

"Okay." Noelle shrugged. "So can I?"

"I need to check with her mother." Ethel pushed to her feet. "Allie, where's Skye?"

"Sam took Skye and Brady down to feed the ducks. He said they'd be over here in a bit."

"Okay. Thanks. Looks like you can sit here with Josie and enjoy some quiet."

"Oh." Allie sent Josie an apologetic look. "I'd planned to ask if I could sit with Sailor and her dad."

Ethel scanned the area. "They're over there talking to the pastor. Why don't you ask them to join us?" She glanced at Josie. "That is, if Josie doesn't mind?"

"Of course not. The more the merrier."

Allie, a pretty girl with auburn hair and sparkly green eyes, grinned. "Thanks. I'll check with them and be right back."

She hurried off to talk to the youth pastor, Caleb, and his daughter.

Josie had met the single dad during her

interview weekend and had enjoyed his out-going personality. She felt comfortable in his presence and was sure he'd make an interesting dining companion.

Gram dusted off her jeans. "I better fol-low Noelle and verify her plans. I'll be back shortly. I need to check on everyone after I speak with Jennie's mother. Enjoy the quiet. It won't last long." She winked.

"I'll be fine." Josie disliked quiet. She missed her big, boisterous family and looked forward to living with the pregnant teens at Lullaby Landing, the newly built home for unwed mothers. She'd signed on to work with them as a counselor and live-in house mother.

She settled back against the sturdy tree. Her eyes followed Allie's long youthful strides as the teen headed toward her friend. She looked to be around six months along in her pregnancy.

The girls chatted and hugged, then turned to Sailor's father. He glanced in Josie's direction, grinned, and nodded. The trio headed her way.

"I understand we've been asked to join you, is that right?" Caleb dropped down beside Josie without further invite. His large presence, both in enthusiasm and stature, invaded Josie's space, but she didn't mind.

His nature and personality reminded her of her older brother, whom she already missed.

She realized Caleb was staring at her, waiting for a reply to his question. "Oh, uh — yes. Ethel sent Allie to offer the invitation."

Josie marveled that she could sound both uneducated and overly formal within two sentences.

"Great. I'm beat." He jostled Josie over with a gentle nudge and stretched his legs and folded his arms. Then he leaned back against the tree trunk and closed his eyes. "I've been up since dawn. If I fall asleep, wake me when the food is ready."

"Daddy!" Sailor hissed.

Josie glanced up and saw that Sailor had stopped at the edge of the blanket. The pretty teen wore her long blond hair pulled back in a ponytail. She stared at her father with wide blue eyes that matched his.

Caleb opened his eyes and looked at her with a grin. "What?"

"You can't just *invade* Miss Josie's bubble and then go to sleep like that."

He frowned up at his daughter, but when his blue eyes met Josie's they twinkled with teasing. "Miss Josie? Am I invading your bubble?"

"My bubble?"

"Your bubble. Your personal space."

"Well, to be honest, considering all the blankets spread around us, you are a tad bit close."

"So you'd like me to move?"

Josie realized she didn't. He'd already mentioned being beat. If she made him move he'd have nothing to lean against. "I think the tree trunk is plenty wide enough for the both of us."

"If you're sure."

"I'm sure."

"So your bubble is intact?"

"My bubble is fine." She patted the blanket beside her. "As a matter of fact, there's plenty of room for a couple more."

She smiled up at the teens.

"That's okay, we'll sit over here." Sailor chose the farthest blanket from her father.

They watched as the girls walked over and settled in. They talked quietly out of Josie and Caleb's range of hearing.

"Sailor doesn't want me anywhere near her bubble." Caleb stated the words with a casual air, but Josie could tell Sailor's reaction bothered him.

"It's an age thing. Not many teens want their parents hovering over them."

He raised his eyebrows and narrowed his blue eyes. "I don't, nor will I ever, 'hover,' " he said in an exaggerated drawl. "The teens in my youth group have trained me well."

"I'm sure they have. I'm just saying that all kids want to distance themselves from their parents. It's a part of growing up and away."

"I don't like this growing-up business." Caleb sighed. "One minute she's a munchkin tagging along on youth events, begging me to let her participate even when she was way too young. She didn't even care about the teens — though she always liked their attention — she just wanted to be with her old man. Now that she's old enough to belong, she doesn't even want me to be on the same continent with her."

"I'm sure it's not that bad." Josie laughed. "She'll come around."

"You'd be surprised, but I hope you're right." He made a growling sound and turned to her. "Enough about me and my daughter, you could probably write complete psychiatric journals about our dysfunctional relationship. I'd much rather talk about you. So" — he shifted so he could better face her direction and leaned a shoulder against the tree trunk like he had all the time in the world — "tell me about Josie Alvarez."

She laughed at his drama, but his perusal

made her feel like a bug under a microscope. "There's not that much to say. I left big-city Dallas and my overprotective family to settle in small-town America and work in a pregnancy center." She flicked an ant off her leg. "That's pretty much it. But to be honest, I'd much rather dissect your and Sailor's relationship. It sounds like it would make such an interesting story. Besides, dissecting other relationships is what I do best. And it's icing on the cake to get excellent research for some journal articles in the process. You just gave me a great idea for supplementing my income. I can write some articles for relationship journals."

"Ah yes. The committee agreed that you'd need some extra cash to make ends meet." He shifted and looked at her with those clear blue eyes. A shock of gold-streaked brown hair tumbled across his forehead before it tapered gradually at the sides of his face and dusted his collar in the back with a slight curl.

His laid-back personality and surfer good looks gave him the appearance of not being much older than his students, but Josie knew he had to be at least in his mid-thirties to have a daughter Sailor's age. Sailor looked to be sixteen or so.

"Are you finished with your examination?

Did I pass muster?"

Josie's hand flew to her mouth. "I'm so sorry!"

"I know, hazard of the career."

"Not really." Josie grinned. "Hazard of my upbringing. Way before I became a therapist, I grew up in a family of people watchers."

"People watchers, huh?"

"I know, sounds weird, right? But we loved to go to the mall and parks and festivals so we could watch people and study their personalities. I think that's what ultimately led to my fascination for studying the various natures of those around me."

"See?" Caleb smiled. "I just learned something about you, and it wasn't all that painful, was it?"

Josie realized he was right. "You tricked me into talking. You're good. I'm the one who listens to others talk about themselves."

"You've met your match with me, then." Caleb's grin was infectious. "My specialty is getting people to talk. Teens are notoriously tough, as I'm sure you know. Maybe we can share trade secrets."

"Sounds like a plan." Josie loved the idea of having an ally when it came to working with her teens. "A lot of my work is done under patient confidentiality, but I would love to have a sounding board in some situations."

"We'll have some of the same kids under our care. Some of your girls are in my youth group. We'll work close together, and I'd appreciate help in some of our youth situations, too. Only with proper approval of course."

"Of course."

"I'd love it if you'd consider helping with the youth group. We can always use more hands."

"I need to get a part-time job first. I'll have to see what my work hours are before I can commit. If it works out, I'd love to help."

"About that — I happen to have a part-time opening at my candy shop *La Dolce Vita.* Would you be interested?"

Josie perked up. "Very! What would I do?"

"Run the register, sell candy, make candy; you'd be a jack-of-all-trades."

"Sounds sweet."

Caleb groaned over her lame joke.

"Sorry, I couldn't resist."

"A few of the older ladies from church take over during youth activities, so you'd be free to help out whenever you want to."

"That's nice. I bet they enjoy the socialization."

"They do. They call it their gossip stop. Whenever one works, the others follow along. It turns into quite the party."

"I can imagine." A few of Ethel's friends from church — Ginny and a couple of others — had taken her under their wing ever since she'd agreed to take the counseling position. The transition went fast — Josie had already given notice at her other workplace and was visiting with family when the job offer came through. Ginny called multiple times to tell Josie about the area and offered her a room at her nephew, Seth's, bed-and-breakfast until the pregnancy center was ready to open. Ginny was constantly asking how they could help as far as getting Josie settled in. Since Josie's hours at the center would be limited as final preparations were being made, she'd enjoy having the job to keep her busy.

"Stop by tomorrow if you want," Caleb said, "and we'll talk about hours and responsibilities. I'll show you around the shop. See what you think."

Josie couldn't wait to see the place. "I'm sure I'll like it. I'd love to work with you, and I look forward to getting to know Sailor better. I appreciate the offer, Caleb."

"Sailor works at the shop, too, so you'll have plenty of time with her. I think it'll be a great arrangement. Right now the two of us are juggling candy-making with customer service, and it can get kind of hairy at times."

"You keep busy?"

"Tourist season definitely keeps us hopping. I'll warn you, some days can be completely crazy, and we can barely keep up. And others are slow as molasses, and we have more candy made up than we know what to do with."

"You can always eat it," Josie teased. "Or is that a bad thing for a future new employee to suggest?"

"I'm sorry to say, but by the time summer is over, you'll be so sick of chocolate and sugar that you'll wish you'd never stepped foot in the place. Hazard of the job."

"Never!" Josie feigned horror. "I can't even comprehend such a thing."

"You'll change your song after eating, sleeping, and breathing chocolate for a few weeks."

"Sounds like a dream job to me."

Caleb rolled his eyes. "I guess you'll just have to see for yourself."

"See what for yourself?" Ethel walked up and lowered herself down on the blanket. She wafted her hot-pink paisley blouse with one hand and fanned her face with the other. "Somebody turned up the heat."

"Caleb offered me a job at his candy shop."

"Oh, you'll love working at La Dolce Vita!" Ethel gushed.

"He says I'll lose my sweet tooth if I work there."

"Nonsense." Ethel laughed. "I've worked there off and on for the better part of a decade. I've gained many a pound thanks to Caleb and his wonderful candy."

"Whoa!" Caleb waved his arms in surrender. "Since when is it my fault that you have no apparent willpower and can't resist temptation?"

"You send me home with a box of my favorite candies every time I leave the place!"

"You make that sound like a bad thing now, but when we're at the shop, you all but tackle me if I don't have the box ready and waiting."

Dinner was announced, and everyone thronged toward the food tables.

Sailor and Allie stood to join them.

Allie hesitated at their blanket. "Are you coming, Gram?"

"I want to catch my breath and cool off first. I think I'll wait a bit and let the line die down."

"Me, too." Josie had no desire to step into that moving mass of bodies again, only to stand in line under the hot sun while waiting her turn.

"I'll come along." Caleb jumped to his feet with the energy of a teen. "Why don't I grab a couple extra plates and bring some food back for you two?"

"Fine with me." Josie could get used to being waited on.

"Don't forget to hit the dessert table if you do," Ethel called as he hurried away.

Caleb laughed and answered over his shoulder. "It's not like I don't know where to get some sweets if the table gets emptied before you all get anything."

He hurried off to join his daughter. Josie smiled. She'd made the right choice by coming to Lullaby.

TWO

Josie rolled over in her luxurious bed at the inn and squinted her eyes against the early morning light. She tried to get her bearings. The unfamiliar room blurred under her scrutiny.

Her eyes were drawn to the outer wall where a gentle breeze blew in from the slightly opened window and stirred the tropical-themed curtains of her temporary room at the Lullaby Bed-and-Breakfast Inn.

She hugged her pillow and smiled. The day that lay before her held a lot of promise.

The job interview at La Dolce Vita took precedence over everything else, but that appointment wasn't until early afternoon. Josie had hours to explore her new hometown before she headed for the shop.

First on the agenda was a thorough exploration of the lake. Josie figured if she was going to live so close to something that caused her so much fear, she'd best confront it from the start.

As future resident therapist for the new pregnancy center, Lullaby Landing, she needed to set an example for her girls. If that example meant dealing with her phobia of large bodies of water, then she'd deal. Or at least she'd try to deal. She'd be living on the lake, and she needed to make peace with it.

Josie slipped out of bed and headed for the bathroom. The attached private bath was every bit as luxurious as her room. Soft blue walls surrounded cool white tile floors. Josie longed to take a soak in the oversize, white marble Jacuzzi. The sunken tub was flanked by scented candles in pastel hues, and the aroma of lavender permeated the room.

At home Josie had always shared a room with her sister, Alexandria. While they'd gotten along for the most part, Josie had always wanted a room of her own. Even though this room was temporary — she'd move to the pregnancy center sometime in the next few weeks — she planned to savor the feeling of being pampered every moment that she was here.

She slipped off her gown and stepped into the large glass-enclosed shower. The bath could wait until evening. Elegant bath soaps and shampoos lined the small shelf inside the shower stall. Josie knew she could easily get used to living like this.

She took her time in the shower then dressed in a peach, cap-sleeved T-shirt and tan cargo shorts.

Josie headed downstairs, following the savory scents from the dining room that lured her across the wide front hall. She passed through the arched doorway and entered the spacious dining room. The bed-and-breakfast was in the middle of a major remodel, and while several rooms were still works in progress, the dining room was finished. Dark-red wallpaper gave the room an elegant feel, and a large oak table welcomed guests to sit and enjoy the atmosphere and meal.

"Good morning!" Miss Ginny greeted her. She was the bed-and-breakfast owner's aunt and a member of the church that had hired her for the center. Ginny had welcomed Josie like an old friend upon her arrival.

"Hey, Miss Ginny." Josie, not sure what to do, waited for further instruction. She didn't want to abuse her status as temporary guest.

Ginny's hands were enclosed in large kitchen mitts. She carried a steaming glass casserole dish to the buffet. She slipped it into place on the gleaming wood surface next to several other containers and platters filled with succulent-looking food and turned to appraise Josie with motherly eyes. "You look much better than you did when you dragged into town a few days ago. How did you sleep last night?"

"Wonderfully, thanks to you! My room, the bed — everything is amazing. I can't thank you enough for letting me stay here. You're sure I'm not putting anyone out?"

Ginny waved her off. "We wouldn't think of doing anything else. We know the budget is tight for the pregnancy center, and letting you stay here until your suite in the living quarters is ready is the least we can do. There was no reason for you to continue your stay at the motel."

"I appreciate it more than you know. The accommodations here are so much nicer."

"Hurry on over and get a plate of food before my nephew gets here. He's out and about working on things, but he'll head in soon enough. You can sit here, of course, but the morning is so beautiful, I suggest taking your breakfast to the patio out back, where you can eat while looking out over the water."

Josie shuddered then remembered her newly formulated plan to overcome her fear of water. "Thank you. I think I will."

She placed a pastry, an apple, and a good-sized spoonful of the egg-and-sausage casserole on her plate before grabbing a cup of coffee and heading outdoors. The buffet offered several other choices, but she figured she'd best pace herself. If she ate everything that was offered, she'd be rolling out of the bed-and-breakfast when she moved.

She walked down the short hall that led to the back door and stepped out onto the patio. The area was bathed in morning sun. Ginny was right. The weather was beautiful — crisp and sunny while missing the heat of the previous afternoon. She supposed the temperature would rise along with the sun, but for now it was pleasant and peaceful on the back porch. She settled onto a padded seat at a whitewashed table and took a bite of the pastry. The cherry turnover melted in her mouth. She closed her eyes and savored it.

"Aunt Ginny makes a mighty fine breakfast complete with her signature baked goods, doesn't she?"

Josie jumped at the nearby voice. Ginny's nephew Seth stood just behind her holding his own fully loaded plate of food.

She nodded. "I've only had the turnover, but if all her cooking is this good, I'll be waddling my way over to my new job at the candy shop." She blushed. "That is, if I'm hired."

Seth laughed. "I don't think you have anything to worry about on either count."

"I hope not." Josie laughed, too, and motioned to the empty seat next to her. "Care to join me?"

"I'd love to." He placed his plate beside hers and settled in so they were both facing the water. "You're talking about the job at Caleb's candy store, right?"

"How'd you know?"

"Small-town living. You'll get used to it."

"Oh." She smiled. "I'm not from a small town, but I suppose the experience isn't much different from growing up in my crazy, gossip-loving family."

Though she'd grown up just outside Dallas, each town bled into the next, so even the smaller towns had blurred boundaries. "Neighbors where I'm from rarely spoke to each other, but in my family news about one member traveled like a wildfire in a field of dry wood."

"Yep, that's Lullaby. We might be full of tourists at various times of the year, but the fabric that holds us together is tightly woven."

"I'll enjoy that."

"Most of the time." The words rolled out on a soft chuckle.

A comfortable silence settled over them as they ate. Josie surveyed her surroundings. The green lawn sloped gently toward the lake. The far-away hum of a boat motor mixed with the closer sounds of circling birds calling to each other near the dock. And the small waves of lake water gently lapped against the wood pilings. The dock was flanked by a couple of jet skis, a large pontoon boat, and a smaller, sleeker speed boat.

"I appreciate your letting me stay here until my rooms above the clinic are available."

He glanced up from his plate. "Like I said, we stick together around here. You're welcome for as long as you need to stay."

"Aren't I displacing other potential guests? Paying guests?"

"Since we're in the process of remodeling, most of the rooms aren't available. I don't want guests here with all the racket going on, so we're just letting a few regulars who understand the situation pass through. As long as you can stand the work crews, you're welcome to stay."

"I haven't even noticed."

"I'm trying to do most of the work during

30

the day when everyone is out and about. The main rooms downstairs are ready. I'm just finishing the upper guest suites and the kitchen. That type of thing."

"Well, don't tiptoe around on my account! I won't mind at all if you need to get work done."

He laughed. "I'll keep that in mind. So far there's been plenty of other quieter work to keep me busy while you and Cameron are around."

"Oh." Seth had laid low and kept quiet for the most part for the short time she'd been at the inn, and she was pleasantly surprised to see this laid-back, comfortable side of him.

"By the way, you're welcome to take any of the boats out when you have a day or afternoon free."

Josie choked on the melt-in-your-mouth bite of casserole she'd just eaten. "I'm sorry. I can what?"

"The boats." He motioned toward the sleek vessels lined up along the dock. "You're welcome to use them whenever you want."

He grinned at her reaction, obviously misreading it as excitement over the generous offer.

"Oh. That's really kind of you." Josie

fought off a fleeting moment of panic. "But I don't know the first thing about boating."

"I could show you. It's easy enough. And if you end up working and spending time with Caleb and his daughter, he can show you, too. He has his own collection of watercraft docked behind the candy shop."

"I — uh — I see. Maybe I'll take one of you up on it at some point, but for now I'd better get moving." She stood and reached for her plate.

Seth motioned for her to leave it, so she folded her napkin and placed it on her empty plate. She picked up the apple and turned to leave.

"The offer stands, whenever you're ready. Just hunt me down, and I'll hook you up with everything you need." He surveyed her, a question in his eyes, but he didn't push.

"Thanks. I appreciate the offer." Josie smiled and waved. "For now, I think I'll take a stroll downtown and walk off this wonderful breakfast as I play tourist."

She liked Seth a lot. His friendly manner put her at ease and reminded her of her brothers back home.

A few hours later, Josie stood outside the candy shop and studied the taffy display in the large plate-glass window. Calico-lined baskets filled with colorful, flavored taffy sat in rows on shelves placed strategically around the edges of the display. Small signs told which flavor was in each basket; peppermint, banana, strawberry, and chocolate were the few Josie could see from her vantage point. A large taffy-pulling machine churned away in the center, whipping up a large batch of the airy confection.

The process seemed to mesmerize the small group of tourists that had gathered around the window to watch. Several small children tugged at their parents' shirt tails and begged them to enter the store for a treat.

Josie grinned at Caleb's savvy business plan. The mouth-watering taffy enticed people to enter the establishment so they could see what other surprises and goodies waited inside. The glass door opened, and the mouth-watering scent of chocolate and sugar wafted out as a couple of patrons strolled out of the building. Josie couldn't wait to go inside, but first she stepped over to study the display window to the right of the entrance. The right side of this window was lined with shelves full of huge chocolate-and-caramel candy-covered apples, several varieties of fudge, chocolate-covered cherries and strawberries, and a

large selection of fancy hand-dipped chocolates. Josie felt like she'd gained a dozen
pounds just standing there looking, and
with a smile said a quiet prayer for strength
and willpower as she contemplated the
temptation awaiting her on the other side of
the glass.

The crowd dispersed. Some of the tourists went inside, and others continued their
window shopping at other locations down
the sidewalk. More tourists drifted her way
and filled the first group's space at the
window, and a new gaggle of children
pleaded to go inside.

Josie took advantage of the lull and hurried into the shop. Cold air blasted her, a
welcome change after the rising tempera-
tures outside the door. Sailor stood at the
counter, and Caleb was busy ringing up
orders at the cash register. So much for their
plan to meet after lunch when things were
slow. Then again, for all Josie knew, this was
slow.

Caleb waved between customers and
motioned for Josie to have a look around.
She wandered around the displays of divin-
ity and pralines. A fudge-making table
rested behind a glass partition lined with
different flavors of fudge. Josie assumed
patrons could watch as Caleb or Sailor

made the fudge throughout the day, too. A large mixer churned behind the table, mixing up a batch of what looked to be peanut brittle.

Josie laughed over the fact that she'd spent more than half a dozen years training to be a psychologist, just to get excited about working at a candy shop.

She loved her career, but even after being in the profession only a few years, she could tell the vocation would quickly take its toll on her. She'd had her fill of counseling couples on the verge of divorce and rebellious teens and hurting children, and while she knew God approved of her choice, she was quickly figuring out she didn't like the negativity of the career. She hoped the pregnancy center would hold off the burnout she'd been experiencing in Dallas.

The fact that the pregnancy center arrangement was only a part-time job that allowed her to supplement her income by doing something fun encouraged her that it would work out. If it didn't, she'd research other professions, like working with youth in other fields, and find something like Caleb's career as a youth pastor or a children's minister, where she could use her degree in a more uplifting atmosphere. She figured God had it all covered without her stressing over it. An added bonus was that Caleb had asked her to help with the youth group, too. She rested in the knowledge that God had a plan in bringing her here, and she was excited to see what the plan was.

Josie pulled herself from her musings when Caleb waved her over behind the counter. Sailor gave her a quick smile before hurrying over to help the next customer. Josie followed Caleb as he led the way through an opening between the displays into a large, open food-prep area. "I'm glad you showed up. I figured the crowds would chase you off."

"Hey, I might not have worked retail before, but I know enough to realize crowds mean the profits stay steady and the work-day flies by."

"Ah, a businesswoman after my own heart, and you've only just walked through the doors!"

She glanced around at the trays of good-ies waiting to go out. "You better wait and see how much of those profits I eat up before you jump to any conclusions. Every-thing looks so good!"

"I'm telling you, after the first week you'll hate the smell of chocolate." His blue eyes sparkled.

Josie already shook her head. "Not gonna

happen. Not even a remote possibility. I'm committed to my chocolate."

"Dad, I need you in the front!" Sailor sounded exasperated.

"You can poke around back here if you want or follow me out front, and I can show you what we do behind the counter." He peeked around the opening. "It looks like we have plenty of customers, so you can probably do both."

Josie did as he suggested and quickly explored the candy-preparation room, making note of what supplies were where and how the various candy trays were stationed. After checking out the storage rooms she headed to the front. Caleb handed her a black apron with the shop's name embroidered in teal and pointed at the sink in the corner. Josie hurried over to wash her hands before joining him at the counter.

"I think we've slowed down enough for you to give us a hand." He grinned. "So what do you think? Are you in? Do you want to work at this madhouse?"

Sailor excused herself to replenish the trays in the display window.

"I'd love to work here. Isn't it every child's dream to grow up and work in a candy factory? This is the next best thing." She rubbed her hands together in anticipation.

"Alrighty then." His expression of pure enjoyment when she said yes lifted her spirits even more than the job offer. He called over his shoulder to the back room. "Sailor, can you take over the second register? I'll work with Josie over here."

Sailor reentered the room and slid a tray of chocolate clusters into the glass-fronted case and moved to the other register.

A customer walked up to Caleb's end of the counter. She pointed at the chocolate turtles. "I'd like four of those for starters."

Caleb grabbed a piece of parchment paper and placed four candies on a scale to the side. "What else can I get you?"

The woman rattled off the rest of the order while Josie watched and learned. After the candies had been selected, Caleb chose an appropriate-sized box and placed the candies inside. He secured the flap and slid a teal ribbon over the box and nestled it to the side. The box looked fancy enough to give as a gift.

"It's just beautiful," the tourist gushed. "I'm taking it home to my neighbor as a thank-you for her watching over my house."

"Well I'm sure she'll enjoy it." Caleb showed Josie how to ring up the order. The woman paid then turned to leave. Caleb called out to her, "You have a great afternoon, and have a safe trip home."

The door closed behind her, and Caleb turned to Josie. "That's about it. Think you can handle it from here?"

"I'm sure I can."

Josie spent the rest of the afternoon and early evening learning and stepping into her position. She already loved the job. She enjoyed chatting it up with the tourists, and she loved meeting the locals. Sailor and Caleb sparred and joked with each other while they made candies, and she couldn't wait to try her hand at making candies on her own.

A loud motorcycle pulled up to the curb around four while Caleb was in the back room. Sailor slipped her apron off without a backward glance. "Tell my dad I'm out with Brian, okay?"

"You'd better run back and tell him yourself." Josie didn't want to be put in the middle of a father-daughter situation, especially not this early in the game.

Sailor hurried out like she hadn't heard, but Josie knew better. She watched as the teen slipped a leg across the motorcycle and pulled on her helmet. She wrapped her arms tight around the boy's midsection, and they rode out of sight.

No one else was in the shop, so Josie peeked her head into the back room. "Sailor said to tell you she's out with Brian."

Caleb's face darkened into a scowl. He glanced up at her and pushed a wayward strand of brown hair from his forehead with the back of his forearm. "She knows she's supposed to check with me personally before she leaves."

"I suggested the same, but she took off anyway."

"I'll talk to her about it later." He sighed as if he suddenly had the weight of the world on his shoulders. "I don't like it when she spends time alone with him like this."

"Tell me if I'm out of line and you want me to butt out, but she's growing up, Caleb. You have to give her some space, or she'll shut you out completely."

"I know. And I'm fine with supervised space. Group dates. Youth activities. But I've told her I don't want her taking off without letting me know where she's going. She knows better. I just lifted her grounding — what we call "restriction" — from last time, and she jumps right in to do it again."

Josie had to agree that it wasn't a good idea for Sailor to take off like that.

Though she was just getting to know them, she hoped the job opportunity would provide the chance to help Caleb and Sailor find a workable plan of action, a way to help

40

them solidify their relationship before
Sailor's rebellious choices pushed them
further apart.

THREE

"Josie? You like my dad, right?" Sailor rested her arms on top of the prep table, studying her, watching for her reaction.

Her casual, offhand question was easy for Josie to answer.

"Of course I like him. He's a really nice guy, and from what I've seen in my short time here, he's a wonderful boss." Josie lifted the cream-filled candy she was working on from the pan of melted chocolate coating and gave it a little twist. Caleb had taught her how each candy had a different swirl or decoration on top so they could easily know what the chocolate coating hid inside. "He's fun to work with and easy to talk to. I can't imagine working anywhere other than here with the two of you. I feel very blessed."

"Well, I know he likes you. *A lot.*" Sailor paused. "I mean, I think he *likes* you, likes you."

Josie laughed and gave Sailor a puzzled look. "There's a difference between liking someone and 'liking, liking' someone?"

"Sure there is." Sailor's high ponytail bounced as she quickly turned her head to smirk at Josie. "I mean, lots of people like each other, but then there's the 'like' when someone likes someone that extra amount, ya know?"

"I think I follow. Anyway, I'm sure your dad *likes* knowing the shift is covered, and that he can trust me to be on time, and that I can do my job without a lot of direction." She'd only been on the job a few days, but already she knew it inside out.

Caleb had trusted her enough today to leave her alone with Sailor while he ran to the bank. Though in all honesty, even with Sailor's quirks and issues with her father, the teen was efficient enough to run the place on her own with or without Josie's help.

"He does appreciate you. He tells me that, like, daily." Sailor rolled her blue eyes, so like her dad's. "That's not what I'm talking about. It's more than that." Sailor licked her finger after she placed an unusually messy confection on the parchment-lined baking tray to cool. "Oops, Dad hates when I do that."

She hurried over to the sink to wash her hands. She continued speaking over her shoulder. "Dad's more chill when you're here. He has a peace about him that he hasn't had lately. He's not as stressed-out all the time."

"Which fits right in with my statement that he's appreciative that I'm here to take some of the load off."

"Because he *likes* you, likes you." Sailor enunciated the words with a smile and waved her wooden spoon like a wand to accentuate her words. A flying strand of melted chocolate landed on Josie's apron.

"I see why your dad chose black." Josie crinkled her nose at Sailor and sent her a forgiving smile. Then, with a quick glance toward the front, she wiped the chocolate off with an index finger and licked the creamy goodness from her finger.

Sailor laughed with delight as Josie took her turn at the sink and washed up. The girl really was pretty when she lit up like that. Unfortunately it seemed that Sailor was sullen and moody more often than happy and carefree. Now the teen leaned a hip against the counter as she watched Josie dry her hands on a paper towel. "So, do you like him back? I mean, in that way?"

"Girl, I've only just met him! I think you

have it all wrong." Josie said the words with a laugh but felt herself blush over the direction their conversation had taken. She'd be mortified if Caleb walked in while they were talking. She realized Caleb's daughter was ruthless and wasn't easy to distract when she had her mind set on something. Sailor was on a single-minded quest to get the answer she seemed determined to hear.

"And I'm telling you I know my dad, and something's different about him when you're around." She resumed her dipping alongside Josie. "I'm not complaining, mind you. Dad's been happier, which makes me happier."

"Why do you say he's happier? He's always been in a pleasant mood when I've been around him."

"My point exactly." Sailor twisted her chocolate with a flourish and placed it on the tray beside Josie's. She dropped another piece of cream fondant into the chocolate mixture and spooned the chocolate over it. "He whistles all the time now. He tells more corny jokes — which I hold you personally responsible for, and that part isn't necessarily a good thing." She pointed her wooden spoon in Josie's direction as she made the accusation, but this time she was careful not to let loose with the chocolate. "His jokes are never nearly as funny as he thinks they are, which annoys me immensely. And he knows they annoy me and takes great pleasure in telling them when he's in this kind of mood. Anyway, that aside, I've seen him get this goofy grin on his face at odd times, usually right after your name comes up. When I ask him about it he denies that anything is different from usual, but his eyebrow quirks up at the corner and quivers in this sheepish way he has when he wants to act like he has no clue what I'm talking about."

Josie couldn't help but laugh out loud. "You're nuttier than that tray of chocolates over there on the cooling rack."

Sailor narrowed her eyes. "I don't think that's a very nice thing for a therapist to say."

"Here, I'm not a therapist. Here, I'm a chocolatier."

"There's a name for what we do? And even more weird, you already *know* that term?"

"Yep there is, and yes I do."

The shop's front door opened, and Caleb's off-tune whistle announced his arrival.

"Told you," Sailor whispered.

"Doesn't mean a thing," Josie whispered back.

Caleb walked through the opening to the prep area. His whistling abruptly stopped as he saw the two females staring at him. He glanced around at the mess they'd made. He shook his head and passed on through to his office. Right before he made it to the door he turned quickly around.

"Hey Sailor, did you hear the one about the man who —"

"Da–*ddy*. Puh–*leeze*." Sailor squeezed the sides of her head with her hands. "Argh. No. More. Jokes. Seriously! You're driving me crazy!"

She stomped from the room, but at the last minute she turned and sent Josie a pointed glare. "Like I said. Your fault!"

"Why is she blaming you for my bad jokes?"

"Ask her." Josie felt the flush returning.

She glanced up to see his eyebrow quivering just as Sailor had described. She quickly returned her attention to the chocolates before she laughed out loud at Sailor's apt description of Caleb's pathetic not-guilty look.

He resumed whistling and headed into his office. As soon as the door closed, Sailor slipped back into the room. "Is the coast clear?"

"He's taken his jokes and left the room, yes."

"Well, I just proved my point, or rather Daddy did. So, you admit now that you see what I'm talking about?"

"I admit nothing. Your dad is a good-natured man, and he seems happy. That's what I see."

"Well, I'm telling you he's happy, and that's not natural. Something's up. And whatever it is, we need to make sure it keeps happening."

"And how, pray tell, do we do that?"

Sailor glanced at her father's closed office door. "Brian and I want to go out to the lake tonight for a bonfire and cookout. Daddy will say no. But if I tell him *you're* going along, I think he'll say yes. He'll want to spend time with you, and you can keep him occupied while I spend time with Brian. Perfect arrangement, don't you think?" Her lips formed into a charming smile.

"It's a perfect plan assuming I want to spend more time in your father's company."

Sailor's face fell. "You don't?"

Josie considered the request. "Actually, I'm fine with it. Talk to your dad and see what he says. If he's game, I'll go along, too."

"Oh Josie, thank you!" Sailor threw her arms around Josie in a rare display of affection. "Thank you, thank you, thank you!"

"You're welcome." She hugged the exuberant girl back. "Just make sure you run the plan by your dad before you talk to Brian."

"I will." She hurried toward her father's office. "I promise to ask him right now."

Josie slipped out of the candy shop midafternoon and headed down a few doors to the clinic. The front door was unlocked, which meant that either the construction crew was inside perfecting the finishing touches on the upstairs living quarters or that Cameron was working in her office and preparing for her next few clients.

Cameron's soft voice speaking from behind her office door and the sounds of workmen on the second level told Josie she was right on both counts.

Josie used her key to let herself in to her private office and placed her purse and a soda on the desk. She checked her messages but only found memos from the director, Brit, and a couple of referrals from Cameron of girls that needed to set up appointments. Though the live-in section of the facility wasn't quite up and running, they'd already started seeing clients during their morning hours.

Josie had set up evening classes for the handful of girls who'd contacted her — group sessions where they could encourage each other and share their experiences as they moved through the unfamiliar waters of being a pregnant teen. Josie hoped that the girls would form a sort of support system and stand by each other at school or meet up during their free time.

Cameron poked her head around the doorway. "Hey, I thought I heard your door. I was hoping to see you this afternoon."

Josie motioned her into the room.

Cameron sank down into a comfy arm chair that sat opposite Josie's desk. "We have three new girls that need private appointments with you. I gave them information on the group meetings, too."

"Thanks. I appreciate it."

Josie and Cameron had hit it off from the start. They'd chatted on the phone a few times over the past couple of weeks as they discussed their first few ideas on how to best work as a team at the clinic.

Cameron, the nurse-midwife, would see the girls through the medical aspect of their pregnancy and would deliver the babies at the nearby birth center or the local hospital if there were complications during delivery. Josie would serve as a support by counseling each girl throughout her pregnancy and helping her decide whether or not she wanted to raise her baby on her own, or whether she should consider adoption. She'd also be present at the birth for the girls who wanted someone there but had no relatives to hold their hands or offer support. She and Cameron would co-teach the parenting and birth classes.

Josie had met several of the girls. She liked them all, but so far she had the hardest time with one aspect of her job. As a wannabe mother with a ticking biological clock, it bothered her to see teens, who weren't ready to parent, nonchalantly come in pregnant without a clue or a care when it came to raising a baby. She knew not all teens had a lackadaisical attitude, but the few who did really drove her to distraction.

It wasn't that Josie didn't have a heart for the girls or compassion. She did. But she could also imagine the difficult life these babies would face if their moms didn't see the importance of their position. She'd seen a lot of tragedy in the city when it came to unprepared teen mothers. Some had left their babies unattended out of desperation while they went out, others took the babies out partying with them, and a few others abused their children out of immaturity or an altered state of mind from drugs or drinking. Most of the time these mothers lost custody. It was sad all the way around.

While those cases were a small minority of the many, many young mothers Josie had seen or heard about at her former practice, the numbers were still there. Even one situation like that was one too many.

One teen in particular, Mandy, was especially difficult for Josie to deal with. So far Mandy was the only client who caused Josie to see red. Mandy was far too thin. She didn't seem responsive to Cameron's instructions to eat better and more often. She was vague about her living conditions, saying only that she moved around from one family member to another. She'd sat sullenly through the first couple of meetings with Josie. Mandy was a prime candidate for the live-in aspect of the center, but the facility wasn't quite ready for her.

Josie hoped that with time and effort, Mandy would open up to them. She hoped that she could get her to agree to move in upstairs, where Josie could better monitor her food intake and could provide the nutritious meals the girl so badly needed. And Cameron would also be right downstairs to keep a watch over her as the days went by.

Though Josie understood the dynamics of girls like Mandy, a part of her wanted to shake the girl for seeming to care so little about the baby she was growing. For that matter, the depressed teen didn't even seem to care about herself and her own health and well-being. It was a dangerous situation for a mom-to-be.

Immediately on the heels of that thought, Josie felt ashamed. She knew God had put her here to help these girls, not to judge them. Josie uttered a prayer of repentance over her attitude and for the direction of her thoughts and vowed to keep her focus on her job. She knew that her purpose was to help the girls get through a tough place as unscathed as possible.

One thing she believed wholeheartedly was that babies were always a blessing from God. Josie's purpose was to help these young teens see that and to help them make the best choice for their baby and for themselves.

Cameron was watching Josie's inner battle with curious eyes. "Want to talk about it?"

"Isn't that supposed to be my line?" Josie laughed. "I'd hate to speak my thoughts out loud. I'm not proud of them at the moment."

"Try me."

Josie explained her feelings, and a look of understanding passed over Cameron's delicate features. Her blue eyes clouded with compassion. "Trust me. I understand more than you know."

"I'm here to help them. Instead, I'm judging them. I know it's wrong."

"You saw Mandy this morning didn't you?"

"Yes." Josie knew the single word said volumes.

"If it helps, I can tell you her baby appears to be fine and is growing normally. I know it makes you feel helpless to see teens like Mandy come through here — it affects me the same way — but we can only do what we can do, and then we have to let go and pray that God protects both mother and baby when we aren't around. We'll make ourselves crazy if we dwell on the girls too much."

"I know." Josie sighed. "Such wise advice. Again, I should be saying those very lines to myself. But I worry about her."

"I do, too. And I will continue to, as you will, as long as we're working with her. That's a hazard of our professions. But we can work together to make things better for her and to see that her baby gets everything he or she needs. This is the whole purpose of the clinic and center, and I feel sure that God put this all together to help Mandy and all the other girls. Girls like her need us more than anyone. I mean, think about it. Most of the pregnant teens have family that might not be too happy with the situation, but they rally and support and provide what the girls need. The Mandy types in the area are the ones who slip through the cracks and don't have anyone or anything. They most likely got into their present situation by looking for someone to love them because they're lonely. In return, they've made their lives even harder. Who wouldn't be depressed?"

"Again, you're telling me things I already know and shouldn't have to be reminded of."

Cameron reached over the desk and gave Josie a quick hug. "I know that . . . and so do you, but I'll need the same pep talk in various forms myself over the next few months and — God willing — years. That's why I'm so glad we have each other, and that even with the limited funding, they voted to take us both on. We need to be a team to help the girls like Mandy. When we burn out, we need to uplift each other as a reminder of why we're doing what we do."

"Speaking of low budgets, how are you doing with the new job at the hospital?"

"I'm enjoying my time there. I've been able to meet the physician who is overseeing my midwifery practice, and we're building a friendship that will help when we need to work together on tough cases. He seems to respect me and my position and fully accepts me as a team player. He and his wife have even invited me over for dinner."

"I'm glad to hear that." She sent Cam a devious grin. "And what do you think about our kind and generous Seth — Innkeeper extraordinaire?"

Cam grinned. "He's gorgeous, and as you already mentioned — kind to boot. I have to say, I haven't met many men like him of late." Her grin disappeared and was replaced with a frown.

"If you don't mind me asking — you were divorced recently, weren't you? Is that why you moved here? To get a fresh start?"

The cloud that passed over Cameron's face darkened. Her blue eyes flashed as she unconsciously pulled her long, wavy hair over her shoulder. Josie thought it looked like she was trying to hide under her cloak of sun-kissed hair.

"We didn't have a good marriage even in the best of times. Jim was a physician, and I was training in his clinic. We hit it off from the start, but even back then I should have noticed his distance and manipulative ways."

"Hey, you deliver babies; you don't analyze people. Even I misread people far too often."

"Well, he swept me off my feet, and I loved the attention. I guess I'm not so different than the teens we were just talking about. I was away from family and friends. I had no time to make new friends other than the few students in my group. We studied and worked all the time. I was lonely. Jim and I married quickly, and only after the fact did he clarify that he never wanted children." She sent Josie an incredulous look. "I mean, can you imagine? The man devotes his life to bringing precious baby after precious baby into the world, yet he doesn't want one of his own. I had no idea."

"The topic never came up during your premarital counseling?" Josie couldn't resist asking. She wholeheartedly supported premarital counseling but guessed from Cameron's first comments that she and her husband hadn't taken time to get any.

"Yeah right." She shrugged. "Looking back now, I know we should have put the brakes on, and we should have had some counseling. Not that it would have mattered. Jim is a master manipulator and would have convinced the counselor and myself that we'd get through any roadblock that came our way."

"Is he a believer?"

"I'm ashamed to say he isn't." Cam shook her head. "Again, I saw the warning signs and ignored them. He went to church every Sunday, served on all the right committees — I convinced myself that even though he didn't talk about his spiritual life, he was one of the private types — but it turned out his activity was all political. He didn't ever show any growth or love for the Lord from his heart. He didn't live for the Lord. He didn't live by biblical standards once we'd left the church doors. It was all for show."

"I'm sorry." Josie didn't know what else to say. Cameron appeared to already know all the issues she'd walked into, and the relationship was already over. "If you ever want to talk more about it, I'm here."

"Thank you. Trust me, there will be future issues. He left our marriage without a backward glance. I know I'll need to talk to you about things as they come up, and I'd love your insight and advice as I deal with some of them. But not right now. For now I'm sure you need to get some things done, and I'm off to meet with my last patient of the day. And Josie?" She hesitated. "For now, can we keep my failure in my marriage and my divorce private? The committee who hired us knows about it, but I'd rather not have everyone else in town look at me as a failure or divorcée."

"I would hope no one would judge you for such a thing, but I understand how you feel. I won't say anything. It really isn't my place. Besides, counselor-client privilege right?"

"Right." Cameron's smile was genuine and filled with relief. "Will I see you at dinner?"

"No, I've agreed to help Caleb chaperone Sailor and her boyfriend, Brian, at a bonfire as soon as they stop by for me."

"Ah, a bonfire! Maybe sparks will fly — and I'm not talking about between Sailor and Brian *or* from the actual fire."

Josie raised an eyebrow. "I'm not sure I pictured you as the matchmaker type."

"Just because I was careless and got burned doesn't mean I can't strike a match in the future. But it doesn't sound like I'm the one matchmaking. Sounds like Sailor and Caleb are already up and running with that one."

"Sailor anyway. Her dad doesn't like for her to be alone with Brian, and she knew he'd say no to the bonfire. She had the great idea that if I went along and gave her dad a diversion, she'd have a better time. I'm not sure on either account, but we'll see."

"You don't think you can turn Caleb's head?"

"Turn his head? Oh for Pete's sake, you sound just like Sailor!"

"And the counselor ignores the question. Interesting."

"Didn't you have a patient to see?"

"I haven't heard the outer door. We have time to finish this chat. It's much too interesting to walk away from."

Just as she spoke, the bells on the outer door chimed and announced someone's arrival.

"Saved by the bell, but we'll revisit this conversation at another time." Cameron sashayed toward the lobby and sent Josie a knowing look. "For the record, I have complete and total faith in your ability to turn his head."

She laughed and closed the door before Josie could say anything else.

FOUR

Josie finished up her office work and headed upstairs to check out the workmen's progress, hoping to get a quick peek at her new quarters before Caleb and Sailor arrived to pick her up.

She was delighted to see the Sheetrock was taped and puttied, and the walls were ready for painting. She couldn't wait to get into her private quarters. Even though she'd soon share the second floor with a dozen or so teen moms, she'd still have her own suite to retire to at the end of the day. She'd be accessible for the girls, but self-contained with a combination sitting room and kitchenette, a full bath, and a bedroom. She'd been asked her color preferences right down to the carpeting. After sharing rooms with family for so long, she couldn't wait to be in her own space.

The inn provided her with a wonderful place for her transitional period, but she longed to be able to shop for herself, to put away her few groceries, and to plan dinner to suit herself whenever she felt like eating. She flung open the double french doors that opened out onto a nice-sized balcony. The balcony overlooked the lake behind the building. This would be her private deck — a place for a table and chairs, a quiet space for breakfast, dinner, or devotions. A wall separated her half from the girls' side. She made a mental list of items she'd need to furnish the small apartment and deck when she had the chance to make it her own.

She heard the soft ding of the doorbell as someone entered the premises. She gave the area one more quick glance before hurrying down the stairs. At this rate they'd be able to accept girls into the live-in program in the next couple of weeks.

Caleb stood ready and waiting at the door, his large stature looking out of place in the small, tropically decorated waiting room. "How's it looking up there?"

"Very nice." Josie grabbed her purse from her office and locked the door. She hurried over to try Cameron's door before locking the outer door, too. Everyone had gone home for the day. "I think I'll be able to move in next weekend."

"We'll enjoy having you as a neighbor."

Caleb and Sailor lived in a loft-style apartment above their candy shop.

"I'll enjoy that, too. I can walk to work at either job."

"You'll love the little market at the end of the street. It's easy to get to for your shopping. We have a small handcart you can borrow anytime you want — I always leave it on our back porch."

"That sounds nice. From the looks of things, I won't even need my car unless I'm going on an outing like the bonfire tonight."

Caleb shot her a strange look.

"What?"

"We don't need a car for the bonfire."

"Oh."

They entered the candy shop, and Caleb locked the front door behind them. The CLOSED sign was already in place, and all the lights were out. They passed through the shop and kitchen and stepped onto the back deck.

Sailor called out to them as soon as they cleared the back door. "Hey Josie! I'm glad you could come. Hurry up, you two, while we still have some light!"

Josie's heart plunged. Sailor stood at the bow of a sleek fishing boat, and Brian stowed gear toward the stern.

"We're, um" — Josie licked her lips and

tried to clear her suddenly tight throat — "we're taking the boat to the bonfire?"

"Yeah. Isn't it great? There's nothing like watching the sunset while out on the water." Caleb didn't appear to notice her change of mood. He took hold of Josie's elbow and led her down to the dock. "The best bonfire sites are reached by boat. There's a small island in the middle of the lake where we prefer to do our bonfires."

"Oh. I — see."

Caleb glanced over at her. "Are you okay?"

She shook her head.

He stopped walking, concern etched in his features. "I'm sorry. We're so used to doing this, I didn't even think about giving you more details. I figured Sailor would have clued you in."

Josie tried to get a grip. She wanted to tell him she wasn't fine, and she'd need to go back to the safety of her room at the inn, but one look at Sailor's panicked face changed her mind. She wasn't going to ruin this night for everyone else just because she had a fear of water. She'd convinced herself earlier in the week that she needed to face that fear, and this looked to be the perfect time.

"It's just that I'm not a big swimmer."

Caleb smiled his relief. "Oh, we can take

care of that. I have life jackets, and you can wear one if you'd like."

Josie's anxiety meter dropped a few notches. She'd be fine. She'd have a life preserver on. Even if, God forbid, something happened to the boat, she'd float until help came.

"As a matter of fact, we'll all wear them since its getting dark."

"Da–*ddy*!" Sailor's familiar moan filled the dusk.

"I'm serious, Sailor. If the boat were to strike a rock or something on the way home or whatever, you know it's best. We've grown too lax on this. And if it makes Josie feel more comfortable, well . . ." He nodded Josie's way.

Sailor seemed to register his unspoken meaning. *If Josie was comfortable, everything was a go. If she wasn't, she might go home, and Sailor and Brian would be at Caleb's mercy.*

Josie almost laughed at the battle that crossed Sailor's features as she mulled over Caleb's insinuation.

"Here, Bri. Wear a life preserver." Sailor couldn't have sounded more morose about the process if they'd canceled the outing.

Brian grinned up at Caleb. "No problem, Captain."

65

Caleb clenched his teeth. He helped Josie onto the boat, and she stiffened as the vessel rocked under their weight.

"It's fine. You aren't going anywhere. This old girl is as steady as a rock. She might feel a bit tipsy, but she'll keep you safe. I promise."

Josie wanted to hold on to Caleb's promise, but how well did she really know the guy? She'd only worked for him for a few days. She figured his status at the church gave him brownie points, but that didn't mean he was invincible.

She sat in the seat he directed her to and settled in. She bowed her head when Caleb fired up the engine, and Brian and Sailor busied themselves with untying the lines. She prayed for their safety and for her fear of the water. Being on the water during the daytime hours was hard enough, but with dusk fast approaching, they'd be coming home in the dark. She knew she'd have to trust both God and Caleb to get her through this ordeal.

Sailor slipped up beside her. "I owe you big time, Josie. Thank you so much for coming along."

Josie could barely hear her over the engine.

"You owe me more than you know," Josie muttered.

"I'm sorry I didn't tell you about the boat. I didn't even think about it. At least you're dressed appropriately!"

"Well, yeah. I figured a bonfire called for casual clothes. This is what I wore to work, you know."

"I know. But still, I can tell you're kind of nervous. Just relax and have fun. Daddy is an excellent captain, and I promise you'll have fun if you just let yourself."

"Once we get back on dry land, I'll let myself."

Sailor laughed and went to the helm to stand beside her father. Caleb stepped away from the wheel and let Sailor take over. Josie gasped as Caleb came to sit beside her.

"She's awesome at driving the boat, Josie. She's been in training since before she could walk. She used to sit on my lap and help me drive as a toddler. I wouldn't do anything to put any of us in danger."

Josie didn't want Caleb to see what a total wreck she really was. "I'm fine." Her voice came out as a squeak.

"If you're so fine, how come you're clutching the seat as if your life depended on it? You look like you fear bouncing right out of the vessel. Your fingers are white." Caleb's rumbling voice was close to her ear. He forced her hands to let go of the seat cushion and wrapped an arm around her shoulders, anchoring her firmly in place. His grasp felt solid and strong, and for the first time, Josie released a normal breath.

"I'm sorry. I have this thing about water."

"Really?" He feigned surprise. "I would never have guessed."

She rolled her eyes.

"So, therapist, what is it about the water that bothers you?"

"Up until I was five, I swam like a fish, and we spent every spare moment at the area lakes and the beach. But just before my sixth birthday, my aunt — my mom's sister — drowned in a lake. It was at a family event and traumatized everyone who was there. My mother promised we'd never go to a lake or a body of water again, and she kept that promise. We never had swimming lessons after that or anything."

Caleb's eyes clouded over. "I'm so sorry that happened to your family. But I don't understand why your mother would prevent you from getting safe in the water. That's exactly what can cause another tragedy to happen. You all should have had swimming lessons and continued with water safety throughout the years so you could prevent another accident."

"I agree, now, but she's drilled her phobia

into our heads from such a young age, we didn't dare cross her."

Caleb sat silent for a moment and stared off toward the setting sun. "You need to learn to swim again, Josie. I'll teach you. We'll go somewhere safe where you can touch bottom and feel confident. I'll let you lead when it comes to what you're comfortable with. But you live on the water now. Many of the activities we do as a church, a youth group, a town, and a family center around the water. If you don't want to face your aunt's fate, you really do need to learn to have confidence in the water."

Josie's heart sped up. She tried to keep the panic out of her voice. "I know that in my head. And I've been praying about facing this fear. But I'm so scared."

"I won't let you down, Josie." Caleb clasped both her hands in one of his. "You'll be safe with me, and I promise we'll take things slow."

"Hey!" Sailor interrupted.

Startled, Josie looked up at the teen. She noticed Brian had taken the wheel.

"Who's supposed to be chaperoning who here?" Sailor put her hands on her hips, and her expression looked just like Caleb's when he was getting on her.

Josie couldn't help but laugh. The sound

bubbled out of her, even on the heels of their conversation.

"Oh hush, and get us to the island," Caleb's big voice boomed. "Some of us are starving back here. Let's get this party started."

Based on the serene smile Sailor sent her way, Josie figured she was doing a fine job of keeping Caleb distracted.

The island was small with a narrow beach all the way around it. A dense collection of trees stood watch from the middle, and a swim area welcomed them to shore.

"All the locals use the island at various times," Caleb explained, "and we try to have several youth outings here every summer. We had one when school let out in early June, and we'll have another just before the start of school."

The boat motor quieted as Brian slowed the vessel to go ashore.

"I'd like to do one more sometime in the next few weeks, but with the float trip and then the Branson trip, I'm not sure we'll be able to fit it in."

"Float trip?" Josie pictured everyone tied together to float along the lake. She knew that was one trip she wouldn't be joining them on.

"Oh, Josie, you have to come along!" Sailor piped in. "We have so much fun. We all take canoes down the river, and we camp out overnight. You'd love it."

"I don't think —"

"Let's wait and see how quickly you take to the water after you have a few swim lessons," Caleb intervened. "I have a feeling you'll be unstoppable in the water, once we get you feeling safe."

"Fair enough," Josie agreed to prevent a heated conversation from starting up. If Sailor and Brian found out she couldn't swim, she'd probably find herself in the water within the next few moments, fully clothed. She'd much rather take her time with Caleb at the helm — and in private.

Sailor kicked off her flip-flops and hopped down into the calf-deep water. Brian handed her a bag of groceries, and she headed off toward the bonfire ring that was already laid out with wood.

"We have a process here where you use what is waiting then prepare the bonfire ring for the next person when you're finished. There's always fallen wood around, and people regularly chop more when it gets low. We have to bring or find our own kindling, but so far we've never come out here to find the area lacking."

71

"That's nice." Josie loved the way the townspeople all stuck together.

She followed Sailor's lead and slid her feet from her sandals. She stopped short of jumping into the lake.

Brian had entered the water, and Caleb was unloading the cooler into his waiting arms. After Brian waded ashore and put the cooler by the groceries, both he and Sailor returned to carry the chairs. Caleb handed down four long canvas bags with shoulder straps, and the couple again splashed their way ashore.

"Looks like we're up." Caleb stared at Josie.

Josie in turn stared at the darkening water. "I can be quite content just sitting here, watching the fire from afar, supervising the kids so they don't feel we're breathing down their necks. We could watch the stars appear one by one. . . ."

"Nonsense." Caleb swept Josie up into his arms and swung his legs over the edge of the boat, causing it to rock. He slid off the edge and kept his grip on Josie as he splashed into the water. Josie screamed and clutched onto him for dear life until he whispered that the kids were staring, and they weren't setting a very good example. Mortified, Josie loosened her grip and allowed Caleb to lower her legs and steady her in the water. The water barely covered her ankles.

"We're good." She waved at Sailor and Brian. "Carry on, kids."

" 'We're good?' " Caleb echoed. " 'Carry on?' What exactly do you want them to 'carry on' with? I'm not sure I want Sailor 'carrying on' with Brian at all."

"Oh goodness . . . my mind is mush. I can't believe I just said that."

"It's okay." Caleb grinned. "I do tend to have that effect on women."

Josie punched him in the side. "I didn't mean my mind was mush because we — because you — I mean . . ."

"Yep, you're at a loss for words. Go ahead and just say it, because I held you close in my arms, and it has you all muddled. Typical, too."

"I'm not *muddled* just because you held me in your arms. I mean, you assisted me from the boat. It's not like it was a romantic moment or anything."

"Looked mighty romantic to those two, I'd assume."

Josie looked over to where Sailor and Brian still stood with their mouths hanging open.

"Way to go Miss Alvarez! Mr. Jackson! I

didn't know the adults could break that six-inch rule."

"Why not? I catch you both breaking it all the time," Caleb growled, "and not for the innocent act of helping a lady off a boat."

"Point taken." Brian quickly busied himself with the bonfire.

Sailor and Caleb had gone to gather kindling, so Josie busied herself with setting up the chairs and chatting with Brian. He didn't seem like a bad kid. He spoke with intelligent sentences, and said he liked his classes for the most part. He wanted to go to college after he graduated. He worked full time during the summer and part time during the school year. Josie wasn't sure why Caleb didn't seem to like the boy, other than the fact that Brian liked Caleb's daughter.

Josie settled into her chair when Caleb started the fire. Small waves slapped against the island's sand. For the first time ever, Josie let herself fully explore the lake's edge with curiosity instead of fear. The setting sun cast an orange glow across the water. The lower edge of the sun had already dipped behind the rolling Ozark Mountains. The town looked like a toy village where it nestled at the foot of the green hills.

The water reflected the graying clouds,

and a few white birds still skimmed the surface, looking for a late-evening meal. Here and there across the water a fish would jump and break the flat mirrored reflection before flipping back in. The water fanned out in circles where the fish entered.

She stood and walked over to the water's edge. She could see the smooth stones at the bottom through the shallow, crystal-clear water. She bent to pick one up. The cool water closed over her hand, and she had to let it still before she could once again see the stone that had caught her attention. She stood and looked at the small, shiny gray pebble and smiled.

Any child could do what she'd just done — and probably every child she knew did exactly that if they weren't plowing haphazardly through the water's edge, splashing with glee. But for Josie, this was a huge move, to actually approach the water's edge and voluntarily break the water's surface to find the treasure that waited beneath.

"If you'll trust me with that rock for a short time," Caleb said, "I can use it for a surprise. Something I know you'll like when the time is right."

Josie jumped. Her musings had been so deep she hadn't heard Caleb come up behind her. She glanced over her shoulder.

Brian and Sailor were roasting several hot-dogs each on long sticks over the roaring fire. Caleb had laid out the other supplies and food items on a blanket he'd spread in front of the chairs.

"Okay — I guess." Josie took one last look at the rock and handed it over to Caleb. She wondered what he could possibly want with it.

"Trust me." He slid it into his pocket and grinned.

"I do. That seems to be a recurring theme with you tonight."

"It's a recurring theme with me always. Trust and faith are the foundations of what belief is built on. We have to trust the Word of God as being true and infallible, and our faith helps us trust God as our Father."

"I agree." Josie didn't know what Caleb had in mind for her rock, but she figured it wouldn't hurt to wait and see.

FIVE

Sailor exited the changing room of the local indoor community pool with her usual air of confidence. Her hot-pink tankini was a testament to their compromise in the swimsuit department earlier in the summer. Sailor had begged and pleaded for a two-piece that was so tiny it could have doubled as an eye patch, while Caleb insisted the cuter choice was a nice, chaste, old-fashioned one-piece. In the end they each reluctantly agreed on the tankini, which covered as much skin as a one-piece.

Josie exited at a much slower pace, her reluctance seemed to permeate her very being. She wore board shorts and a rash guard over her swimsuit, a life jacket over those, and carried every floatation device known to man.

Sailor rolled her eyes and mouthed *good luck* to him then headed for the diving board at the deep end.

Caleb hauled himself out of the water and walked over to stand dripping at Josie's side. "I see you bought out the entire floatation-device department over at the general store. The tourists will be disappointed."

"I left plenty for them." Josie's accent was more pronounced than normal, and she avoided looking him in the eye. "And I'd be more than happy to give the tourists these 'floatation devices,' as you call them, and be done with this whole ordeal."

Josie's snarkiness made him smile.

"This 'ordeal,' as *you* call it, could some-day save your life. You need to learn to swim. You live in a lakeside community now." Caleb held firm to his stance. "What do you say you lose about ten pounds worth of equipment and join me in the shallow end?"

Josie startled and jumped as the diving board thudded, and they both turned to see Sailor execute a perfect jackknife into the water. Josie glanced at Caleb and visibly shuddered. "Or we could watch Sailor perform her death-defying tricks into the pool, and pretend I'm safe on shore for the rest of my life."

"Nope. Not gonna happen. It's too dan-gerous for you to be out *on* the water — or even living and driving around it — without being safe *in* the water."

"I was afraid you were going to say that."

"C'mon, walk over to the steps with me."

Josie let him take her arm but didn't drop any of her gear.

He led her to one of the benches parents used to watch their young ones during swim lessons. "Drop the gear here."

"No." Josie hugged her swim noodles, swim ring, and kickboard close to her chest as if they were her lifelines.

"Josie." He motioned again toward the bench, and Josie reluctantly put down her gear.

She crossed her arms around her midsection. Her stance was more insecure than defensive. Caleb's heart went out to her.

"Look, I know it has to be hard to be a shrink and tell everyone how to overcome their fears while you battle your own, but I'm here for you. We're going to work through this together."

He got the reaction he was going for.

"A shrink, Caleb? Really? That term is so outdated — I can't believe you just used it. I don't refer to myself as a shrink, and I'd appreciate it if you didn't either."

Caleb felt his face redden even as he purposely teased her. He figured if he irritated her, she'd stop feeling nervous and get out there and prove what she could do. But he didn't want to make her completely mad at him. "Sorry. Remember, I deal with teens for a living, and sometimes I can push the wrong buttons when dealing with adults. With the teens it works better to just get it out there and not tiptoe around proprieties."

"Forgiven." Her icy tone melted. "I counsel teens, too, remember, and I know exactly what you mean. It's much easier to talk bluntly to them while we have to tiptoe around topics with adults." She sat on the edge of the bench. "That's why I took this job. I prefer to work with teens."

"I do, too." Caleb pushed aside the pile of floatation devices and sat next to her.

They stared out over the pool. Sailor climbed to the top of the high dive and walked to the edge.

"She's making me queasy just watching her walk up there. I don't know how she does it."

Caleb laughed. "Wait until you see what she does next. She flips and twists and twirls enough to make even *me* a bit nervous. And I've watched her do it since she was little. I think she was created specifically to be in the water."

Sailor did a flipping twist, and Josie dropped her head to her hands and groaned.

She muttered a few words in Spanish before glancing back up at him. "How does she do that?"

He laughed. "Sailor was born part mermaid. I'm telling you, she took to the water as a baby and thrived."

"I can't even imagine."

"Well, you will soon enough. We're going to get you in the water today. You don't have to do twists and turns off the high dive, but you'll be comfortable enough in there that you'll feel safer when you're around the lake or any other body of water."

Sailor swam across the pool and pulled herself up to sit on the edge near their bench. "Are you two ever getting in, or did you come to watch me dive?"

"Yeah, yeah. Give us a minute, why don't you?" Caleb waved a hand in her direction.

She laughed and headed back to the boards. This time she went to the low dive.

Josie drew in a breath. "Where do we begin?"

Caleb admired her sudden spunk. "We'll start right here at the steps. They aren't slippery, so you don't have to worry about that. And the water at the bottom is only a few feet deep. It shouldn't go over your waist. I'll be with you every step of the way, literally."

Josie looked down at her life jacket.

"We can do this one of two ways. You can wear that until you get used to the water, or you can take it off now. It'll help you float, but any security will be a false security. If you fall in the lake, you won't necessarily have a life jacket on. You need to learn to swim without one."

She hesitated before fumbling with the clasps of the life jacket.

Caleb reached over to help. He tossed it on the bench with the other gear and rewarded her with a smile. "Let's go into the pool. Slow and easy now. Let's just take one step at a time and acclimate you to the water. It tends to be a bit on the cold side." He made sure to stay close beside her. He held her elbow and helped her ease down the steps into the water.

Josie's breaths came in fast bursts.

"You're going to hyperventilate. Try taking slow, deep breaths."

She visibly tried to calm her breathing. She stopped when the water reached her knees. "I can't do this."

"You can. You said you swam as a young child, and you weren't afraid of the water. This is your mother's fear — a fear that is totally understandable under the circumstances — but she passed it on to you when your aunt died. You need to learn to over-come it." Caleb kept his voice gentle. "You remember when we were on the boat, and we talked about having faith and trust in God? This is one of those situations. In this case, you need to have faith in me and trust my ability to keep you safe. I'm not going to let you fall any more than Christ does when He's watching over you."

"I want to trust you. It's just that . . . I don't know. I do have faith in God, and I trust Him even though I can't see Him. Trusting a human is a different story al-together. And this is a physical situation. . . . If you let me fall, I'll go underwater."

"I'm not going to let you fall. You won't go underwater. I promise. How about we pray for God's peace to descend while you work on trusting me?"

"It can't hurt." Josie's reply was less than enthusiastic.

"Okay." Caleb chuckled. "I'll pray, and you focus on trusting me."

She nodded.

Caleb prayed for Josie's safety, her confi-dence, and her ability to trust someone with human faults.

Surprisingly, she really did seem more at peace after his prayer had ended. She stepped down the remaining three stairs and stood frozen in the waist-deep water. "What now?"

"Now, you float."

"I float." Her laugh had an edge of hysteria to it.

"Yes. Float. On your back."

"Huh-uh, not gonna happen." All her confidence seemed to fade.

"Sailor! Come here a minute."

Sailor dove in and swam underwater to where they waited. "I need you to give us a demonstration. Float on your back for us."

Sailor tipped back on the water and let her legs drift toward the surface. The water buoyed her up, and she straightened until she floated flat on the surface.

Caleb placed a hand under her back. "See? She can float without my help, but I'll put my hand under your back until you're ready for me to let go."

"You'll be standing there until eternity hits if you're waiting for me to be ready."

"That's funny, Josie. I love your sense of humor." Sailor snickered and stood. She dove underwater and headed back toward the diving board.

"I wasn't joking," Josie said. Her lips turned up in a grin.

"I know." Caleb laughed. "C'mon, let's do this."

Josie moved to stand in front of him, and he wrapped a supportive arm around her upper back.

"Lower yourself slowly down in the water. I'm right here, and I won't let you go under."

"I feel like a preschooler."

She didn't look like any preschooler he'd ever seen. He couldn't help but notice the way the water Sailor had splashed when she kicked off clung to Josie's long black lashes or the way her brown eyes sparkled with mischief when she laughed at herself. And he also couldn't help but notice that even with the rash guard and board shorts, her slender figure didn't look anything like a preschooler's.

She settled back in the water, and Caleb's heart swelled as she lifted her feet and mimicked Sailor's movements. She fully trusted him to be there for her. He was surprised to realize how much that meant to him.

"Perfect! That's awesome! Look at you!" He kept his arm under her shoulders and touched her waist with the other, just enough to stabilize her hips on top of the water. He eased the arm that supported her shoulder away while looking into her face. She stared at the ceiling above them. Her forehead was wrinkled with the effort not to panic. "You're doing it! You're floating. I'm going to slowly remove my hand from your waist. Don't freak out on me. If you feel unsteady or uncomfortable, raise your shoulders up out of the water while lowering your feet toward the bottom of the pool, and you'll be able to stand."

Her nod was barely perceptible, but to his surprise she didn't panic at all. She floated even when he moved his hand away. A beautiful smile transformed her features from worried to content. She gently swayed her arms across the surface, ruffling the water with her fingers. After a few moments she lowered her legs and stood. A flash of panic lit her eyes. He reached out to balance her. His desire to touch her soft skin was again overriding her need for support.

She let out a long breath. "I did it. I remembered! I floated on my own!"

"Yes, you did. You were awesome." He grinned and motioned her to deeper water. "How about trying some swim strokes? Are you ready? I'll support your stomach this time while you go through the motions. Let me know if you feel confident that you can move along on your own, and I'll step away."

Sailor came over and demonstrated different swim strokes, and Josie followed her lead while Caleb supported Josie's stomach. She caught on like a pro.

"Do you think you can put your head underwater?" Sailor caught her dad's enthusiasm. "If you learn to swim underwater, you can get around even faster."

"I'm willing to try. I've forgotten how much fun this is. I had no idea this would be so easy and enjoyable."

"I'm starting to think you're part mermaid, too," Caleb teased. "If I didn't know better, I'd assume you knew how to swim all along, and that you were leading us on when you said you couldn't."

Her eyes widened. "Are you kidding me? I couldn't fake that anxiety. Like I said, I could swim when I was little, but that was about the time I turned six. Since that awful day when my aunt drowned, I haven't so much as submerged a toe in water deeper than a bathtub."

"Agreed. That was too real to be faked."

"I can't guarantee I'll be as confident in the lake."

"I think you will be. If you can swim here, you can swim pretty much anywhere. We'll start with lessons at the lake next. We can go to the island when no one's around, and we'll practice in the shallow water until you feel comfortable."

Caleb worked with Josie on swimming underwater for the next half hour.

She swam with a grace some swimmers never accomplished. She popped her head above the surface of the pool and smiled at him. "A question? Why not practice in the water by our docks? It's shallow enough there, too, isn't it? Why go all the way out to the island?"

"It's shallow enough, but you'll have numerous bystanders loitering around watching if you swim there."

He saw her shudder.

"No, thank you. The island is fine."

Caleb laughed. "We need to get on it because the float trip is coming up fast."

"I won't feel confident enough to swim by then. Not like that."

"We each have a cushion that floats to grab onto if needed. I think with one of those, and your new skills, you'll be ready when the time comes. It's a lot of fun, not something you'll want to miss. And the chances of us tipping are slim to none."

"I want to go." Josie's smile lit up the dim pool area. Without seeming to realize it, she dipped down in the water and half floated, half bounced while pushing off with her feet. She wouldn't have dreamed of doing such a thing a mere hour ago.

88

"You do realize you're bobbing in the water, right?"

"Hmm?" she asked, her voice dreamy.

"You're bobbing in the water. Like a natural."

"What? Oh my goodness! I am. Who'd have thought I'd be doing this today? No life jacket, and here I am enjoying myself. To be perfectly honest, I didn't plan to get my new suit wet when I left the house."

"Well, you surprised us both."

The diving board sounded loudly behind them, and they turned to see Sailor executing another perfect twist.

"This week? Submerging in the water. Next week? Flips from the high dive."

"Over my dead body." Josie dove under the surface and headed for the stairs.

Mandy had missed two counseling appointments in a row, but she managed to make it to the third. She slumped in the seat across from Josie's desk and folded her arms defensively across her chest. Her unwashed hair hung in strands around her face. Her clothes were dirty and sagged on her too-thin frame.

Josie felt her frustration with the girl grow but tried not to let it show. It wasn't Mandy's fault that Josie's biological clock was ticking away. But Josie reminded herself that she didn't walk in Mandy's shoes, and Josie had no clue what the girl went through on a daily basis. She prayed for compassion and understanding.

"Mandy, how's the housing going?"

Mandy shrugged. "Not so good."

"I can't read your mind, honey. I can't help you if you don't communicate with me. Are you still living with your sister?"

"No. We got in a fight — her boyfriend was mad about me always being there or somethin' — and they kicked me out."

Josie held back her sigh. Each time they met Mandy had a similar story. "So where are you living now?"

Mandy looked away. "Here and there."

Josie knew better than to push. If she did, Mandy would shut down or leave.

"Have you given any more thought as to whether you want to keep the baby or place him or her up for adoption?"

"Not really. I have time." She studied her dirty fingernails.

Josie cringed at the thought of Mandy trying to raise a baby on her own when she didn't make the most basic effort to care for herself. But that's what the clinic was there for, to offer help and support to girls like Mandy. She just hoped they'd have things fully up and running before time ran out for this duo.

"We need to have a plan in place," Josie said softly.

"I know, but I can't decide that right now." Mandy's words were angry, but Josie detected a hint of frustration behind them. She had a point. When she barely knew where she'd be sleeping from day-to-day or where her next meal would come from, how could she focus on an event that to her must feel like forever in her future? Right now, her everyday existence was taking all the strength Mandy had.

"Well, try to give it some more thought. The classes I told you about can help. I'd love to have you attend. We discuss options for you and the baby, and you can get input from other girls in similar situations."

Mandy nodded but didn't commit to coming.

Josie continued to try. "If you plan on adopting the baby out, we need time to decide who the adoptive family will be, and we need to figure out how involved you'll be in the process. You have the choice of an open or closed adoption. Those are all decisions that are best made well in advance of the birth."

Mandy picked at a loose thread along the

bottom of her torn and stretched-out T-shirt.

"If you choose to keep the baby, you need parenting classes."

No response.

"Have you eaten today?"

Mandy halfheartedly lifted a shoulder.

Josie reached into her desk drawer and pulled out the sack lunch the chef at the bed-and-breakfast had packed for her. "Here, take this."

Mandy's eyes widened in surprise, and for once she didn't hesitate. She reached for the bag. Her quick look of gratitude said what her words didn't.

"Um. I still need to go see Cameron. I don't want to be late for that appointment."

Josie glanced at the clock. She didn't feel that she'd had time to go over anything important with Mandy. She knew Cameron didn't schedule her appointments this close to Josie's, but she didn't push. She knew all the time in the world wouldn't make Mandy open up to her. Maybe Cameron would make better progress. She tried one more angle. "Do you have any questions for me? Anything you need to talk about before you leave?"

Mandy shook her head and stared despondently at the floor.

"Okay then. Try to make it to class tomorrow night, okay? I think you'd enjoy meeting the other girls, and the classes really do help prepare you for the decisions you need to make."

Mandy looked at her as if she were speaking another language, but even though the girl tried to keep them all at arm's length, something in her eyes pleaded for understanding.

"We're here for you Mandy."

"Thanks." She held up the lunch bag. "And I do 'preciate this."

Josie smiled and wished she could do more.

Mandy headed across the hall toward Cameron's examining room, and Josie checked her appointment book. Mandy was her last patient for the day. She locked her office and hurried upstairs to check the progress of the dorm.

The walls were freshly painted, and all the doors and windows were open to the balmy July breeze. The cement floor had been swept clean in preparation for the carpet that was scheduled to be installed early the next morning. The finishing touches were in place, and in another couple of days Josie could move into her new home. She'd have just enough time to settle in before the youth group's float trip.

She couldn't wait to have her own place, but she suddenly realized how lonely she'd be until the girls moved in. She was glad she'd have Sailor and Caleb nearby.

Six

"Hey Josie! Daddy wants to know where you want your bed." Sailor appeared in the bedroom doorway, hands on hips, awaiting Josie's reply.

Josie slowly eased up from her kneeling position on the hard kitchen linoleum, where she was organizing her new pots and pans in one of the lower cabinets. Her cramped knees rebelled at the sudden change of position.

The three of them had been working for the better part of the day, and while Josie was more than ready to call it quits, she wanted the final touches to be in place so she could just bring over her last few belongings from the inn the next morning and be settled. She wouldn't have been able to do it as smoothly without the help of her friends.

Sailor had spent her time bouncing from room to room, helping out where needed.

At the moment she was assisting Caleb as he put together Josie's new bed frame.

Josie entered her bedroom and frowned. "Oh wow. The bed is larger than I thought it would be. I love the one at the inn, but I guess I didn't take into consideration the difference in room size."

"Queen beds aren't exactly compact, but its not too bad. You still have plenty of space to get around. We just need to know where you want the headboard before we put the foundation and mattress in place."

Josie motioned to the long wall opposite the door. "I think this wall will work best. The smaller spaces can be used for my dresser and chair."

"Your easy chair could go in the corner over there by the french door." Sailor motioned to the tall window that flanked the set of bedroom doors that led to the balcony. She looked nervous as she pulled her blond hair into a high ponytail and then released it again. "You can sit there and read while you look out over the lake. I mean, if you want to."

"I agree." Caleb walked over to stand by his daughter. He rested a casual arm over her shoulder. Sailor responded by reaching up to hold his hand.

Josie could see by Sailor's spontaneous reaction how much the father and daughter cared about one another. She hoped they'd get through the glitches and growing pains with Brian and keep their relationship close and intact. She vowed to help guide them in any way possible through this new experience, as both a caring friend and someone who cared about them professionally.

Caleb glanced over at Josie. "I think Sailor has an excellent idea. What do you think, Josie? Do you want me to put the chair over here so we can see where the bed fits in once the chair is in place?"

"Sure. Sounds good to me." Josie appreciated their candor. She'd never furnished an apartment before. Either Sailor or Caleb had accompanied her on all her shopping trips to gather her furniture and decorations. "I hope you both know how much I appreciate your input and dedication."

She watched as Caleb lifted the overstuffed armchair and maneuvered it into place. It was a perfect fit and created a wonderful reading nook. "Great idea, Sailor! You have a knack for this. I love it!"

"Me, too." Sailor beamed. "And the bed will still fit on the long wall just like you wanted — it just won't be centered in the middle of the wall."

"That's okay. I think it'll look even better

offset. It'll also give me more space to move around on this end of the room."

They walked over and team-lifted the large bed frame in place. Caleb eased the foundation and mattress onto the frame. The room was coming together.

"We just need the dresser in here, and you'll be set as far as this room goes." Caleb walked out with the two-wheeler, and they heard him moving around in the living room.

"Need some help?" Josie called out, knowing he'd tell her no.

"Nope. I got it."

She and Sailor exchanged a glance, and Sailor responded to Josie's smile with a giggle.

Caleb entered the room wheeling a five-drawer chest and positioned it opposite the bed. It fit perfectly next to the door that led into the living room. "What do you think?"

"I think that's the only place left where it can fit." Josie laughed. "If we'd bought any more furniture, we'd be up a creek."

Caleb motioned them from the room. "C'mon. We have another room to put in order."

Sailor hung behind. "Want me to put the sheets and duvet on the bed? I can hang the shower curtain and towels in the bathroom for you, too. That way when you walk in, you'll get to see it all finished."

"That would be wonderful." Josie would enjoy coming into the finished room after Sailor did the final touches. She started to follow Caleb from the room, but something about Sailor's demeanor caught her attention. "Are you feeling okay? You look a little pale."

Sailor rolled her eyes. "I'm fine, *Mom*. I stayed up a bit too late last night, but I'll make up for it by going to bed early tonight." She softened her words with a smile.

"If you're sure. I know we worked you hard today." Josie started out the door but turned around in the opening. "How late is 'a bit too late' if you don't mind my asking?"

Sailor blushed. "Um. Sometime after midnight. I was talking to Brian on the phone."

"Mm-hmm." Josie ducked her head around in time to see Caleb entering the living-room door with her loveseat. She lowered her voice. "I'm not sure your dad would be too happy to hear that. I need to help him get the loveseat through the doorway, but if you want to, you can try out the bed with a little nap after you get it set up. We'll be busy out here for a bit."

"I doubt I'll take you up on that, but thanks for the offer."

Josie could tell Sailor was fighting the urge to roll her eyes again. Josie hurried over to help Caleb get the loveseat through the door. It was small, but it folded out into a twin-size bed, which made it heavy and awkward to move. Josie had chosen it anyway, knowing she'd have family members visit at times, and without a second bedroom the foldout bed would help the small quarters double as a guest suite.

"She doing okay?" Caleb huffed. "I heard you asking if she felt all right. I thought she looked a little peaked today myself."

"She said she's fine. She's just tired, but she said she'd go to bed early."

"Stayed up too late, huh? Probably had something to do with that boy, right?"

"His name is Brian, and I'm not going to be party to gossip."

"Aha, thought so!"

"I didn't say anything!"

"You didn't have to."

Josie folded her arms across her chest and refused to answer further.

Caleb laughed and helped Josie settle the loveseat in place, but all the while he muttered to himself about dating and teens and arranged marriages that didn't happen until after the age of forty. He walked out for the armchair while Josie busied herself back in the tiny kitchenette. With all the help her boss and his daughter were giving her, she'd be settled by nightfall for sure.

"Where do you want this one?"

"I don't have many options, maybe in the corner by this set of french doors, just like we did in the bedroom? With this little eating bar over here, that's about the only spot left."

Caleb did as she suggested. After he had it in place, he stood and surveyed the room. "I think it's coming together nicely. I'm afraid with it being so cozy and all, you'll never want to leave home to come to work."

Josie laughed. "I agree it's cozy and all, and I love the convenience to everything, but trust me, I'll be in for work. I need the income."

"Oh, and here I was waiting for you to say you'd be in because you'd miss my charming personality."

"That, too." She laughed. "And don't forget I'm going to have a dozen pregnant teens living just outside my door. I don't think I'll have a lot of time to sit and enjoy my quiet suite. I might be ready to escape this place more often than not."

"Good point." Caleb shuddered at the

thought. "I imagine it'll be kind of crazy around here most of the time. But hopefully, with each girl having her own space, things will fall into a semi-normal routine once they start arriving."

"I hope so, too."

Caleb glanced around. "I think we've done about all that we can do, short of getting your things from the inn. Do you want me to help with that? We can run over and have your things back here before dinner."

"No, you and Sailor have both done enough. You go home and take the rest of the day off. I hate that you gave up a Saturday to help as it is. Kick back and put your feet up. I'll load my final things from the inn and finish moving in tomorrow. I have another hour or so here to finish up in the kitchen, and then I'll head to the inn and call it a night."

"I tell you what. You finish up here, and I'll fix us a meal out back on my deck. It's the perfect evening for a barbecue. We can all kick back, and you can eat before heading home. We both know the kitchen will be closed when you get back to Seth's place."

"True." Josie smiled. "And how can I resist an offer as good as that?"

Caleb walked over to the bedroom door to tell Sailor and motioned Josie over to join him. They stood shoulder to shoulder in the bedroom doorway. Sailor was sacked out in the middle of the bed. "I guess we did work her pretty hard."

"Mm-hmm. Leave her here, and I'll wake her and bring her with me when I'm done."

"I have a feeling she was up more than 'a little late' last night."

"It's summer, and she's a teen. Don't tell me you never spent late nights chatting it up with Sailor's mom when you were young."

Caleb's only answer was a grunt.

Josie laughed. "Busted."

"Maybe. But in my defense, we were much, much older."

"I'm doing the math, and I don't see how you could have been all that much older."

"It's like cat and dog years."

"It is, huh?"

"Yep. And if you don't understand it, I'm not going to explain it."

"Because there is no explanation. You're grasping."

"I'm not grasping." Caleb made his way toward the outer door as they talked, eyeing his escape. Now he stood on the threshold of making his getaway.

"It's the typical double standard."

"You theenk you know so much. You

theenk you know me so well. You make a me laugh."

"Your fake accent makes *me* laugh."

"I'm outta here."

"Pathetic. Go ahead. Run away. Busy yourself playing with fire so you can forget about Sailor and her late-night calls and focus on making us each a steak or something. Some of us have real work to do."

Caleb darted out of sight down the stairwell with a laugh and a wave of his hand.

Josie hurried down the stairs. In a sudden burst of energy, she skipped the last one and threw open the back door. She couldn't help but smile at the thought of dinner with Caleb and Sailor. They'd accomplished a lot, and while she still had her clothes and essentials to move from the inn and she had some boxes to pick up that she'd stashed in a storage area at the church — for the most part, she was finally settled in her own place. Her first official home in Lullaby.

The pebbled path that curved along the lakeshore called to her, and she hurried down the hill. She had only to walk the distance of a mere two backyards to join Caleb and Sailor on their lakeside deck. With the deck facing east, they had a nice shady area for their evening barbecue.

Josie couldn't help but laugh when she saw the huge fire burning in the barbecue grill. She appraised the fire with a calculating stare. "Should I go for a fire extinguisher?"

Caleb lowered his eyelids and glared. "It'll burn down in a few minutes."

"The flames or the grill?" she teased. "I'm betting on the latter. Do you have the fire department on speed dial?"

"Very funny." He closed the grill lid and pretended to ignore her. He busied himself with organizing his table of grilling accessories. He lined everything up just so. Juicy steaks and hamburger patties, waiting to be cooked, rested on a nearby platter. Hamburger fixings already waited at his side. Lettuce, tomato, ketchup, mustard, pickles — he hadn't missed a thing. Chips, dip, and a pan of baked beans rested next to a cooler.

"All this food is for us?"

"I figured we worked up an appetite. If we don't eat it all, I'll have leftovers already made up for the next few meals." He turned to her with a grin. "Help yourself to a soda."

Caleb was decked out in a red apron with CHEF printed across the front in large white letters. He lifted the lid and stoked the fire. He started putting steaks on the wire rack.

Sailor walked out the back door and put

the finishing touches on the table. She'd hurried home after she'd awakened and realized she'd fallen asleep on Josie's bed. Josie grabbed a soda and walked over to join her. She dropped into a padded chair with a sigh of relief as she popped the tab on the can.

Sailor lowered herself down onto the chair next to her and reached for her own waiting soda. "Tired?"

"Very. But I'm excited about how much we got done. Thank you both so much for all the help. I'll bring over my last load from the inn in the morning, and I'll officially be your neighbor. I look forward to waking up to this view of the lake each morning."

Amusement filled Sailor's eyes. "Don't you have the same view from the inn? I think pretty much everyone in town looks out over the lake in one way or another."

"Exactly. I do have a view, but the inn is set farther back from the water. It's pretty, but I can only see a smidgen of water from my window. The whole backyard is full of trees that block what little view I have, too. Here I'll have patio doors that open onto the deck from each room. These buildings are situated much closer to the lake. I can sit outside and savor the view from up close."

Caleb turned from the open grill to stare at her. "Sailor, reach your hand out and touch her forehead. I think Josie overdid it today, and she isn't thinking clearly. Isn't this the lady who couldn't stand to be near the water only a week or so ago?"

"The one and the same." Josie laughed. "But you two have been merciless about getting me in the pool almost every day since. I have to say, I'm starting to enjoy the whole experience."

"She's enjoying it, Daddy. Did you hear that?" Sailor put a hand to her heart.

He nodded. "More importantly, she's admitting she's enjoying it!"

Sailor and Caleb glanced at each other with raised eyebrows.

Josie rolled her eyes and shrugged.

"So" — Caleb sauntered in her direction while casually flipping the spatula in the air and catching it — "does this mean you're ready to take the next step?"

"What's the next step?" Josie glanced nervously at the lake. It might be pretty from afar, but jumping into a huge body of water similar to the one her aunt drowned in was a whole different ballgame. "If that step has to do with murky water . . . no."

"The next step — the float trip! Can't wait!" Sailor trilled.

Caleb motioned for her to cool it. "We leave bright and early Friday morning, which gives you plenty of time to get settled in here and ready for the big event."

"Is the water murky?" Josie narrowed her eyes. She refused to let go of her question.

"Nah, you'll love it." Caleb waved a hand. "The river's crystal clear. It's filled by freshwater springs and streams."

"On a good day." Sailor giggled.

"Sailor!" Caleb pinned her with his eyes.

Josie looked back and forth between the two. "Murky or clear water? Sailor?"

Sailor glanced at Caleb. Her mirth-filled blue eyes reflected the fire from the grill. "Both?"

"It isn't pool blue except at the swimming hole. But it is clear, and you can see the rocks and pebbles at the bottom of the river, even in the deeper places."

"Unless it's been storming," Sailor interjected.

"And it hasn't been storming, so you're safe," Caleb said. "You'll be fine, Josie. You will truly love it. The scenery can't be beat, you'll be surrounded by fun people, and you'll be in my canoe. You can put your feet up and sunbathe while I do all the work. I promise I'll take care of you."

A thrill ran through her at his words.

She'd enjoy being taken care of for a change. As the oldest daughter, she'd done her share of caring over the years. She hoped he didn't notice her reaction, the small smile his words brought to her lips. "And if we tip over?"

"I'd jump in and rescue you. But we won't tip. I don't ever tip."

Sailor frowned. "Well, yeah, except for that time when the boys ganged up on you and flipped your canoe on purpose."

"Thanks, Sailor." Caleb stared her down. "But that doesn't count. I'll make sure everyone knows there will be no canoe tipping. I think we made that clear last year after they did the deed and ruined all the food. They respected the rule the rest of the trip, but we'll reinforce it this year for good measure."

"Yeah, I guess they did learn a lesson, didn't they?" Sailor sighed as if the thought of not tipping canoes put a bit of a damper on her trip. "But we had fun anyway."

Josie pursued her line of questioning. "Will we have life jackets?"

"We have cushions that float, and you can pretty much touch bottom everywhere on the river."

"Pretty much?" Josie raised an eyebrow.

"I'm sensing some vagueness in your answers."

"Josie — you can swim. You've proven yourself at the pool. Swimming in a lake or river isn't any different. The river's current is gentle. You're going to do fine, and you're going to have a blast. I promise."

"I hope so. Tell me how this floating-cushion thing works."

Caleb groaned. "We tip over — you grab hold of your cushion. It's that simple. You're going to be fine."

"But a cushion?"

Sailor laughed. "Basically you sit on it, and if you start to fall in —"

" 'Fall in,' as in the canoe tips over?"

"Yep . . . if you start to fall in, you grab it."

"So as I fall, I'm supposed to remember — in my panic — to grab my cushion so I don't drown?"

Caleb snorted. "Yes. So when you land in the water that comes up to your knees, you'll be able to float."

"*All* the water will be knee deep or less?"

"Well, no, but the deeper water is the slower-moving water. The odds of us tipping there are slim to none."

Sailor tilted her head, her expression contemplative. "Unless you do something crazy like jump up in the canoe and scream because you see a snake or something. Remember when Sarah did that last summer? It was awesome!"

Josie cringed. "A snake? I hate snakes."

Caleb sent Sailor an exasperated glare before turning to Josie. "You don't like snakes, either?"

"From a distance behind a glass wall, maybe. Not in my swimming hole or the water I'm about to tip over in. No."

"When you get a dozen or more kids in a swimming hole, snakes tend to scatter and lay low."

"I guess you have a point." She was quiet a moment. "What if I fall into the snakes' swimming hole?"

Sailor couldn't hold back her giggle. "This is going to be great."

"If you fall into the snakes' swimming hole, yell out a warning. That'll give them time to steer clear."

Caleb and Sailor bumped fists.

"So do I grab my cushion before or after I yell the warning?" Josie couldn't help laughing.

"During. I'd say yell the warning while you grab your cushion. You'll have to multitask."

"Got it."

"Seriously, you can wear a life jacket if you want, too. By law, we all have to have one in the canoe. They actually prefer that you wear one."

Josie could just picture it. She'd be sitting in their boat, looking like a huge orange overstuffed penguin, while everyone else sat primly on their seat cushions. "Do you wear one?"

"No, and neither do most of the kids." At least Caleb was honest.

Sailor had to jump in. "Try — none of the kids. No one ever wears the life jackets. Although I do think the Doogins put life jackets on their toddlers the year they helped us out."

Caleb reached over and mussed Sailor's hair. "Again, the faster water is the shallow water, so even if by some remote chance we tip, you'll be able to touch bottom and get your footing. The worst that can happen is you'll get a scrape or bruise from the pebbles before you get your feet under you. As for the life jackets, most of the teens choose to use the seat cushions."

Caleb headed back over to his fire and flipped the steaks. One by one he carefully slid burgers into place. He put the pan of beans on the side burner and adjusted the gas temperature control. "We've not had a lot of rain, so the water should be slow and might even be low enough in some place that we'll have to carry our canoes. Make sure to wear old tennis shoes."

SEVEN

"Hey, Josie! Sailor! Glad you finally decided to show up," Caleb teased as he hopped out of the driver's side of a large SUV and waved Josie over in his direction. He walked around to meet her. "You're riding along with me. You can put your purse in the front seat."

Sailor immediately changed course and beelined to the fifteen-passenger van that waited at the curb in front of Caleb's vehicle, but not before she dropped her huge duffle bag at his feet. "Thanks for the ride over, Josie. I appreciate not having to get up at 4:00 a.m. like Dad did. See you at the river."

"Anytime, Sailor. I'm thinking 6:00 a.m. is more than early enough for me, too."

Sailor hurried off to join her friends. It looked like most of the kids had already arrived.

Caleb stared at the large duffle bag,

perplexed. "How can she possibly need that much stuff for an overnight trip?"

"I don't know." Josie shrugged. "You said you were glad we finally showed up. Are we late?"

"No, I'm just giving you a hard time. You're actually early. About half the kids are here. Seems most parents can't get their kids here fast enough. You notice not many waited around to see them off, either."

"They're all heading back to their comfy beds." She yawned and eyed the tent bags that were stacked in Caleb's SUV. Sleeping bags tumbled around the tents in disarray. "We're sleeping in tents?"

Caleb looked at the tents then back at her. "Uh. Yeah. Where did you think we'd sleep?"

"I don't know — maybe a local hotel?"

He laughed. "There are no hotels around the river. The tents are pure luxury. I did toss in a few foam pads to go under your sleeping bag, though. You and Brit will be the envy of all the girls."

"Or we'll be their targets." Josie glanced over at the van filled with teens.

Sailor had just reached it. She disappeared from sight as she climbed in to join her friends in the back.

"Guess she doesn't want to ride with her old man, huh?" Caleb grinned.

"Would you?"

"Oh ya. My dad was the coolest."

"Hmm." Josie placed her purse in front of her seat and slid her overnight bag from her shoulder.

"What exactly is 'hmm' supposed to mean?" He stood with fisted hands on hips. The indignant pose made her smile.

"Just 'hmm.' " She handed over her bag.

Caleb's eyes didn't leave her face as he took her bag and swung it in the side door. He staged it behind her seat. "Look. Easy access. Nice, huh? You'll notice I flipped down the middle seat so we could put the luggage here, and the three kids who are lucky enough to ride along with us will be in the farthest backseat from us."

"Because you really enjoy the kids, right?"

"I do enjoy them, yes, but I'm also a veteran and know that less is more at this point in the trip. After two full days in their company, you'll be thanking me for my foresight and thoughtfulness."

As if to reinforce his comment, three of the younger middle-school boys tumbled out of the other van and headed their way, jostling for position as they walked. The boisterous trio shoved and sang at the top of their lungs.

"Hey, Caleb," the nearest one yelled, "the

big kids don't want us in their van. They said we'd have more fun in here with you."

"Ah, no, no, no!" Caleb muttered under his breath. "Looks like Matt and Brit got the jump on us with those three. I'd hoped to snag Sailor and a couple of her friends to ride along with us. The teen girls can be loud — boisterous even with their singing — but they aren't — these three. When Sailor walked off, I got distracted by you, and now look what's happened." He glanced at her with his usual teasing demeanor.

"So it's my fault?" Josie laughed. "And what exactly has happened?"

"Have you spent any time in the company of those three? Surely you've seen them in action. At youth? They're . . . they're . . ." He shuddered.

"Spoken like such a loving youth pastor!"

Caleb shook his head. "You have no idea what you're in for."

"Maybe I should go ride with Brit and Matt."

"Don't you dare. I need a female counterpart in here with me."

"Why? All the girls are in the other van."

Caleb leaned close. Close enough that she could smell the fresh scent of his soap. "Please, Josie, you can't leave me alone with them like this. Not those three. Please don't leave me at their mercy. I have to focus on my driving. If I have to watch them in the rearview — and trust me, I will have to — there's no telling what will happen. Our safety and lives rest in your hands."

"This sounds like fun." Josie knew he was being goofy, but she also knew she couldn't leave him to ride alone, period. She'd looked forward to this trip and the time spent in his company. The drive over was a bonus she hadn't thought of.

"Hey, Caleb. *Hey,* Josie." The smallest boy shouldered his way past Caleb then stood close to Josie while raising his eyebrows. The other boys shoved him from behind while sending Josie similar flirtatious grins.

Caleb stepped between them. "Boys. GO. Now."

"Sheesh, we're going." The smaller boy climbed in, and the others were close on his heels. They looked like a pack of puppies, jostling for position. A moment later the smaller one tumbled back out, surrounded by gales of laughter from the other two. He stood up, dusted off, and dove back in on top of them.

A minute later a lone voice called out. "Hey, Caleb, why is the seat in the back? How can we talk to Josie if we're all the way back there?"

Josie couldn't tell which boy spoke. The boys still tumbled around in the SUV. They were shoving and wrestling without pause.

"My point exactly," Caleb muttered under his breath. Caleb's smile was smug as he tossed the boys' luggage in and slammed the door. He leaned against it.

Even through the closed tinted windows, she could hear the boys' shouts and see them tumbling and diving over each other.

"Matt owes us big."

Josie nodded. She was already glad Caleb had thought to put them all the way in the back. It wasn't hard to see why they'd been kicked out of the older kids' vehicle. She figured after a few hours in their company, she'd need therapy herself.

Three hours and a pounding headache later, Caleb turned onto the long graveled drive that led to the canoe rental parking lot. "We made good time. We should be out on the water early enough for the long day's float."

"What was the alternative?"

"Half a day. If we'd had to stop a lot, we'd have done an afternoon float instead."

An attendant waved them down and chatted with Caleb before directing them to the campground. Josie slid from her seat. Her limbs were tight after the long drive, and it felt good to stretch. The kids poured out of the vehicles. Several headed for the bathrooms while others gathered around the leaders.

Matt and Brit motioned their group to join Caleb and Josie's small gathering.

"Matt, why don't you and the ladies take the teens down to the river and get them settled while I finish up here? The canoe guys can go over procedure with the kids. Make sure they get their cushions and life jackets, and then you can go over boat assignments while I finalize paperwork." He handed Matt a clipboard with names and canoe partners on it.

Caleb watched as Josie helped direct the teens to the canoe launch area. Her eyes reflected her insecurity as she glanced back at him. He smiled, hoping she'd read his encouragement. He liked Josie a lot, and if they had a future, he wanted her to share his love of the outdoors. They appeared to be polar opposites, but she seemed open to trying new things, and he prayed she'd learn to love the great outdoors as much as he did. If she didn't, he'd adapt.

He hurried through the paperwork and approached Josie at the river's edge. The day was perfect with just enough cloud cover to keep the direct sun from beating down on them. The river, about forty feet across at this point, was flowing slowly, the gentle current lazily pushing the water past where they stood.

"Seems harmless enough," Josie said as he stopped beside her. "Not the roaring Mississippi I'd pictured in my nightmares."

Caleb let loose with a belly laugh. "If that's what you were picturing, no wonder you were apprehensive."

He walked over to one of the canoes and loaded up their gear. He took one cooler for their canoe while Matt took the other. The teens had already tied their gear into their canoes and were securing everything in the waterproof bags they'd brought along.

"Looks like everyone's set and ready to go."

"Yep, as ready as we'll ever be." Josie sounded upbeat, but her fisted hands told Caleb otherwise. He chose not to comment and draw attention to her anxiety.

Caleb told the kids to get in the river. They slid their canoes in with great fanfare and splashes of water. Several of the kids took him literally and went directly into the water. He waited for the roughhousers to move away before sliding their canoe into position. He held it steady. "You climb in the front, and I'll get in once we're fully on the river. Hold the sides and stay in the center of the canoe as you work your way forward. Go slow and get used to the wobble."

She did as he said but gasped when the canoe rocked slightly from her weight.

"You're fine. I've got it."

She settled on the bench and clutched the cushion with both hands.

"Do me a favor and get that paddle from the bottom of the canoe. Put it straight down on the bottom of the river on the deeper side, and hold it steady."

Again she did as he asked. He waded out into the water and carefully climbed aboard. He tried not to rock the boat any more than necessary.

Josie squealed as it rocked a bit more without the vessel being grounded on the shore.

"We're good." His words came out on a chuckle. "Stay centered on the bench, and we'll be off."

He pushed against the water, his strokes strong and sure. Matt and Brit had taken the lead, which left Caleb and Josie to bring up the rear. Some of the more experienced kids fell in behind Matt with strong strokes while others circled around going every which way but where they needed to go.

Brian and Sailor were right behind Matt's canoe.

The three middle-school boys were in the same canoe and kept going in circles. They finally drifted in a straight line but were headed for the opposite shore. Rather than run into it, they tipped their canoe on purpose.

Caleb sighed and called out to them. "Pull it to the shore over there, and get back in. This time, row in unison. If you don't get a system going, you'll wander all over the place. Put your oars in on opposite sides, and switch regularly."

Caleb gave his instructions to various groups, and as the kids practiced and started to understand what he was saying, they drifted downstream one by one until Caleb was able to fall into the rear position.

Josie dared a look over her shoulder. She smiled. "I was wondering if there was more to it than this."

"Maybe we should have done the half day after all." He grinned. "At the rate we're going . . . we'll be all day just getting organized to go the first mile."

He watched as she reached over to trail a hand in the cool water.

"It's cold."

"Remember, it's spring fed. Even in the

hottest weather it feels comfortable or even chilly."

"And the kids will swim in it?"

"Oh, they'll swim all right. And wait until you feel the lagoon. It's freezing, but they'll all go in."

"That'll be fun to watch."

"We won't be watching. We'll be going in, too."

Josie wasn't so sure. While she appreciated his patience and encouragement, swimming in ice water wasn't high on her priority list. She'd worn a suit under her clothes as instructed by Sailor, but if the cool river was any indication, the lagoon would be downright icy. "I'm not sure my Southern blood will allow me to go in water that's colder than this."

"Your Southern blood will adapt. You don't want to miss this."

He was ruthless. She pushed her oar through the water as he'd instructed the kids, and her arms started to feel the burn. She didn't know if her movements were helping or hindering, but she was having fun regardless.

"You have good rhythm."

"Thanks." She pulled the oar from the water and perched it across her lap. Low-hanging trees obscured both shorelines from sight, their branches almost touching the greenish-brown water below. She dared to get a little closer to the edge of the boat so she could look into the water below her. Though the canoe rocked slightly, it didn't tip.

She could see the stones on the bottom, just as Sailor had said. "I see fish!"

Her excited call caused several of the kids in the canoes ahead of them to laugh. One of the girls leaned over to look, almost taking her canoe with her. She quickly righted herself, saving her and her canoe mate from capsizing.

"Casey?" Caleb called. "Next time you want to look over the edge, warn your partner so she can compensate by scooting the other way."

Josie glanced back at him. "Sorry, I didn't know that. I'll do the same next time."

"You don't have to worry about it. You'd have a hard time tipping us if you tried."

"Meaning?"

"Meaning — you weigh about half what I do. Casey and her friend weigh about the same, so her weight's going to affect their canoe differently than yours would."

"Oh." The river narrowed, and she saw movement in the water to their left. A small object headed their way, leaving a tiny wake in the water. "Um, Caleb, is that a snake?"

She pointed at the approaching creature.

"No, it's a turtle. You'll see a lot of those. Look under the trees and branches. They like the low-lying logs and roots that allow them easy access to the water." He turned the canoe and headed for the trees.

"Not too close!" Josie squealed and leaned back. She could see huge spider webs in the trees and had no intention of getting caught up in one.

"I won't go under there. But look" — he pushed backward on the oar and swung the canoe around so it was parallel to the tree again — "see the turtles?"

"I do. Three of them."

They continued on downstream. The beauty reminded Josie of Texas, and she suddenly found herself homesick. The blue sky reflected on the water, and the white puffy clouds passed over the sun at regular intervals. The trees were a vivid green against the sky, some brighter than others. Every once in a while a squirrel would race them down the river, jumping from tree to tree as it hurried along their route.

"Thank you for bringing me along. It's peaceful and beautiful here."

"I thought you'd like it. I'll bring you back

someday without the teens. We could ask Matt and Brit to come along. I don't know what it is, but something about being out in nature makes me feel closer to God."

"Me too, but I never really felt it until I moved up here. When I sat on the patio at the inn or when I stand on my new balcony at Lullaby Landing, I can feel His presence much more strongly too."

They rowed in silence for a while, often letting the current carry them along; the only sound was the oars gently slapping the water. Caleb would sometimes use his oar as a rudder to guide them in the direction they needed to go. At one point tall cliffs surrounded them on both sides.

"It's beautiful," Josie gasped. "I had no idea there were canyons in southern Missouri.

"Well, they aren't anything like the canyons out West, but they are something to look at, aren't they?"

They rounded a bend and saw that the others in the group had pulled off on a sandy shore. Caleb gripped the canoe and catapulted himself into the water. He barely rocked the canoe in the process. He guided them to the beach and pushed the canoe hard, securing it on shore. Matt stepped over and helped Josie to her feet. Her legs were shaky after spending the past couple of hours on the water.

"Why are we stopping?"

"Some of the kids wanted to swim. This is a good beach for it. A few others wanted to take that trail up to a cave we visit every year."

"A cave?"

"Yep. Brit and I were about to join them. Want to tag along?"

"I'd love to."

"I'll stay here and guard the swimmers." Caleb headed for the water. "You all have fun."

The trail led upward for a short while before leveling out and heading along the cliff. A solid metal rail had been built on the outer edge of the path. Several teens stood outside the opening. A small waterfall poured out from the mouth of the cave.

"Can we go in, Matt?" one of the teen boys asked.

"Only a few feet. We don't have flashlights, so only go as far as the light reaches."

"Aw, c'mon, man!"

"A few feet or nothing."

The teens splashed around for a bit then headed back down to the river. Brit, Josie, and Matt stood at the entrance after the last teen had finally headed back down the trail.

Brit took an elastic hair band from her wrist and pulled her dark hair up into a ponytail. "I wonder how far back it goes."

The day had warmed as they'd drifted down the river.

Matt put his hands on his hips and surveyed the entrance. "I don't know. Lots of people know about the cave, but I'm not sure anyone has ever taken the time to explore it."

"We should do it sometime." Josie surprised herself with the comment. The move to Missouri had changed her outlook. She wanted to experience all that life had to give.

"We should." Brit smiled. "I'd love to go farther inside — if we were properly equipped."

They turned to head down the path and found the kids antsy to get back on the water.

Caleb waited nearby. "We'll stop at the lagoon for lunch."

Matt nodded and helped Brit into their canoe before pushing out onto the river.

Boat by boat, the kids fell in behind them. Caleb and Josie again brought up the rear. Caleb didn't speak until everyone was safely in place on the water and drifting downstream. "What did you think of the cave?"

"It's fascinating. This whole area makes me think of the pioneers who first settled here. I mean, did they use the caves as homes until they were able to build something more secure? And the Indians had to have used them at some point, right? Think of the things the walls of that cave have witnessed. I bet plans were made there. Wedding proposals? War councils? Who knows?"

"You have quite the imagination." Caleb's eyes twinkled in the sun. "But I know what you mean."

Again they fell into a comfortable silence and drifted along in the peaceful hush. Birds called from the treetops. The wind rustled the leaves. As the canoe in front of them drifted around the next bend, Josie felt as if they were the only people on earth. She couldn't imagine anything breaking her contemplative mood.

"Rapids ahead!" Matt's voice carried from far around the bend.

Except that. Josie gripped the sides of the canoe. Her oar was all but forgotten beside her. "Rapids? They sound very — fast."

"They won't be much, but we'll have to steer around the larger rocks. If we hit a boulder, we could tip."

"You said we wouldn't tip!"

"We won't. You know how you said you expected the river to be like the Mississippi? These currents are nothing like what you see in white-water rafting in the movies, okay?"

"If you say so."

The current picked up.

"Get your oar, Josie, and do as I say. We'll be fine."

Josie grabbed the oar. She wasn't sure how she could possibly help.

Caleb called out orders, and Josie did as he said. If he said to push hard to the left, she rowed hard to the left. When he said row right, she changed the oar to the other side. They worked as a team and flew through the shallow whitewaters. Two canoes capsized. One held the boys from the SUV. They were arguing and went smack into a boulder. The canoe spun around backward and tipped, dumping the trio into the water. They immediately surfaced and waded over to where Matt had snagged their canoe.

Two of the girls screamed as their canoe made it through the rapids but then headed for the trees at the river's edge. Both ducked to avoid webs in the trees and promptly tipped their boat. They came up sputtering and laughing. Several of the boys waded over and helped right the canoe and gather their floating supplies.

Everyone was accounted for, so they loaded back up and continued down the river.

Caleb grinned at Josie. "You survived."

"I did." She grinned back. "Is that the worst we'll go through?"

"We'll have various forms of the same thing as we go, but yes, the others aren't any worse than this one."

"The boys tipped."

"They were being boys and weren't paying attention. They survived, didn't they?"

"True." She pictured the laughing girls who'd tipped themselves. "The girls almost seemed to tip over on purpose."

"I agree. They like attention. The boys came to their rescue, so all went according to plan, I'm sure."

Josie enjoyed attention, too, but she'd stick to the attention she was already getting from the back of their canoe.

Caleb steered the canoe toward the shore to the left.

"Why are we going this way?"

"The lagoon is just around the next bend. It's easier to go ashore if I angle from here. Matt will be busy catching the kids who miss it. The water speeds up from the spring as it merges into the river, so if you miss the shore you have to backtrack on foot a bit while pulling your canoe. It isn't fun, especially going against the current."

So much to learn. "Gotcha."

He kept them near the shore as the water increased in speed. "I'm betting the rapids gave everyone a good appetite."

"I know I have one. I'm starving, and I haven't even done much of the rowing."

"You've done plenty. I'm impressed."

His words caused Josie's heart to swell with joy. Caleb's compliments, whether over decorated candies or rowing a canoe, were starting to mean a lot to her. They rounded the corner, and the edge of the lagoon came into view.

EIGHT

Breathtaking. No other word could describe the beauty of the perfectly round lagoon. Caleb hadn't even tried to explain how beautiful it was. He had mentioned something about the blue pool, but Josie hadn't come close to imagining how truly pretty this hidden-away treasure would be. If she hadn't been looking, if she hadn't been with Caleb, she would have missed it altogether. The pool was tucked into the bend so discreetly that other than the change of colors in the water where the spring rushed into the river, she wouldn't have known it was there.

Obviously several of the teens *had* missed it judging by the number of kids pulling their canoes upriver on foot.

The lagoon nestled perfectly into the river's curve. The turquoise water rivaled that of any pool, but with the greenery that grew naturally around it, it looked like a tropical paradise. The brilliant blue water formed its own stream as it poured into the river. It merged into a neutral color a few hundred feet down the way. The current was strong, so if you weren't watching for it, it was easy to miss until you were past.

The other canoes were pulled ashore just past the lagoon's opening. A dirt path surrounded the pool, which allowed the teens to spread out and perch on large boulders with their sandwiches.

Caleb jumped out, pushing against the strong current and pulled their canoe high onto the sandy beach. Waiting teens surrounded him and reached for the cooler. Caleb stepped onto the path and started passing out icy-cold sodas. "Remember, leave only your footprints. Trash comes back to me. I'll have a bag hanging on this branch. Got it?"

"Got it!" several voices singsonged in unison as the crowd dispersed. The kids returned to their perches.

Caleb turned to Josie. "Are you getting out of the canoe, or do you want to sit in there while you eat?"

"I'll get out. I'm just taking in the view. It's beyond beautiful."

His smile warmed. "I thought you'd like it."

He helped her from their boat. Everyone had settled in. The younger boys had already finished their meal and now walked dangerously close to the water's edge.

Caleb leaned close. "Who do you think will be the first in? You know they can't stand that close without one pushing the others into the water."

"A sort of repeat of the last stop?"

"Yep. Exactly."

A loud splash proved him right. Josie strained to see around Caleb. No one was left on shore. "They all went in?"

Caleb was laughing out loud. "Yep. Jonah pushed the other two but lost his footing and went in after them."

The older kids were cheering and jeering.

"And I missed it." She didn't mind. She didn't mention that the reason she'd missed it was because she'd been distracted by Caleb's nearness. His broad shoulders blocked her view of the boys, but she'd been perfectly happy looking up at them.

"You'll see plenty more of the same as we eat. First, the boys will start in on the girls. They'll tease about throwing them in. Then one will accidently get thrown in for real. Then it'll be pure chaos while the girls try to get even. No one will be safe. Even you."

Josie stopped walking. "Then maybe I will

136

eat in the canoe. The water is beautiful but deep. I don't want to go in there. I'll just sit in the canoe and observe from afar."

"Too late." Caleb grasped her arm. His gentle touch defied his teasing words.

"I'm serious, Caleb. That water looks way too deep. I can see the bottom — it's truly amazing, but I know I can't touch. I don't want to panic in front of the kids." Her panic wasn't far away and bubbled up through her words.

"I'm sorry." Caleb's countenance changed as his teasing tone disappeared. He rubbed his thumb up her arm, causing her to shiver. "I didn't mean to frighten you. I won't let anyone throw you in. I'll personally stay by your side and protect you. They know better than to mess with me."

"It's okay. You go play with the kiddies; just make sure to tell them not to throw me in, okay? I don't want to ruin your fun. Or theirs."

"I'm having more fun here with you" — he motioned to a large boulder set away from the others, where they could sit and eat their sandwiches — "than I'll ever have goofing off with them."

A piercing shriek announced the entrance of another teen into the water. One of the boys brushed his hands together in glee as his female friend sputtered and treaded water.

The girl glanced up at him. "Oh, you are so dead."

The other guys started razzing him. The boy just stood and grinned at his girlfriend with a goofy look on his face.

Josie watched their reactions. "He doesn't look too upset with her threats."

"Nope. He only hopes she'll try to push him in. That way he'll have an excuse to get close to her and throw her in again."

"Kids."

"I know. Silly isn't it?" He glanced over at her. "But I'd let you push me in."

"No thanks." She couldn't hold back her laugh. "You just hope I'll do that so you can have an excuse to push *me* in. You're just an overgrown version of them."

"Guilty as charged." He looked longingly at the water. "I should be ashamed. You should throw me in for trying."

"You're hopeless!" She took a bite of her turkey sandwich. "But you can go play if you want to. I don't think the kids know me well enough to come after me. I'm safe."

"You don't know these kids at all, do you?" Caleb appraised her. "I like that. You're so innocent in the ways of the wild. It's . . . refreshing."

"They wouldn't — would they?"

"Oh yeah — they would."

"Hmm. Then maybe you should fight them off for me. Keep them distracted so they leave me alone."

"Well, you might have a point there. I might have to join in for a while, if only for that reason. But I'll be watching out for you in the process."

"Good. Because if you don't and they get to me, you'll be one sponsor short on the trip to the amusement park."

Caleb walked toward the edge and spread his arms in reference to all the teens and their riffraff. "Like you could resist another outing with us." In the process he let down his guard, which allowed several of the older boys to body slam him, sending him flying into the cold water. He grabbed hold of the nearest ones and dragged them in with him. He rose up sputtering, and with a roar, sent the laughing boys scattering in all directions.

The game was on with all the kids trying to knock the others in until so many were in the water they could all relax and swim. The few holdouts had made it clear with threats of bodily harm that they weren't to be thrown in.

Josie didn't miss the fact that most of the

teen girls stayed near Caleb. She couldn't blame them. His easy smile, fun nature, and handsome good looks made him an easy target for teen crushes.

Sailor sat alone on a boulder across the spring, knees drawn up to her chest, her expression contemplative. Josie started to walk over to her then thought better of it. If Sailor wanted a few moments to be alone, Josie wasn't going to interrupt her. But she did make note to talk to the teen later that afternoon and make sure everything was okay. Sailor seemed unnaturally quiet compared to the bubbly, fun-loving teen Josie had met a few weeks earlier.

The thought made her think of Mandy. Mandy was quiet and contemplative, too, but Josie hadn't felt the same compassion or concern toward her. She knew she needed to love all the girls equally, but she hadn't. Mandy was the perfect age to attend the youth event, but circumstances — an unplanned pregnancy, poverty, and survival — made it impossible for her to come. Several of the girls at the clinic attended the youth group. Brit's sister, Allie, had come along. How had Mandy felt when she heard whispers and discussions about all the fun they were going to have while she was left behind?

140

Some of the less compassionate folks would say Mandy had it coming — that she'd made her choices, and those choices had repercussions. Josie knew they'd all made bad choices at one point or another. God didn't hold those choices against them, so neither should they stand in judgment of each other.

She felt awful that instead of understanding and coming to such a realization earlier, Josie had judged Mandy and found her wanting. She could blame it on burnout, but she knew better. She hoped Mandy hadn't sensed her judgment. Josie had no idea what curves life had thrown the young girl. As her therapist, Josie shouldn't have felt the way she did toward the girl at all. She dropped her head.

Lord, I'm sorry for my attitude toward Mandy. If You'll give me another chance, I'd like to try harder to win her trust and to build a relationship with her. I'm sorry I let my desire to have a family and a baby of my own overshadow what should be more important — reaching out and building a relationship with her through trust. Trust is all encompassing as I'm learning more and more every day since coming here. Trust in You, trust in Caleb to be there for me when he says he'll be, and trust in Your plan for me and possibly through me — Your plan for Mandy. If I hurt her in any way, please forgive me and let me make it right. Please help me remember that all that I do, I do for You. Amen.

Josie felt better after her prayer. She couldn't wait to see what God would do when it came to helping Mandy. She wished she could head back right then and make things right for the girl. Since she couldn't do anything about Mandy, she decided she'd stop hiding on her boulder and trust Caleb and have some fun for a change.

She slipped off the boulder, feeling brave, and walked over to the side of the spring that had a gentle downward slope into the water.

Sailor rose from her perch and walked over to join her. She looked incredulous. "You're really going in?"

"I think I am." Josie smiled. "Wanna join me?"

"Maybe." Sailor bit her lip.

Josie studied her. "You aren't sure you want to? I figured you were used to this. I thought you'd be one of the first ones in."

"I used to be, but today I'm not so sure."

"Why not?"

"I dunno. I'm just not sure I feel like it."

"How about we both slip in here and watch the others from a safe spot? I'll warn off anyone who comes our way."

Sailor smiled. "Sounds good to me."

Josie stuck her foot in the water and almost swallowed her tongue. The water wasn't just cold; it was icy cold. "This is arctic! How do they get in there?"

"The freezing temperature is why most of them either went in by force or jumped in without feeling it first. That's about the only way to make yourself get in. I've always jumped in like they did in the past, but this year? It doesn't sound as enticing. Maybe I'm growing up and getting a brain." The emotion in her playfully stated words didn't reach her eyes.

"Is everything okay, Sailor? I'm here if you want to talk."

Sailor glanced over to where Brian was talking with some of the guys in the youth group. "Nah. I'm fine."

"You sure? 'Cause I'm here for you."

"I know, and I appreciate it."

Josie waited a moment, but Sailor didn't say anything else. "Is everything okay between you and Brian?"

"Yeah." Sailor glanced his way again. "I mean, I guess so. He's kind of distant right now, but we'll work through it. We always do."

"Okay, so back to the water — what you're

saying is, we won't likely get past our toes?"

"We will, but we'll have to take it slow. As soon as one body part numbs, it's easier to get the next part in."

"Sounds awesome." Josie grinned. She did as Sailor suggested and eased her way into deeper water. "I'm only trying this at all because I'm so hot."

"I know. Heat can make a person do weird things."

"Yeah, stupid things, like climbing into an arctic spring to *relax.*"

"Yep."

Caleb suddenly appeared at the rim of the ledge. "C'mon in, the water's great. Refreshing even."

"Refreshing?" Josie raised her eyebrows. "You might say it's icy even, don't you think? We're standing in it if you didn't notice."

Sailor laughed, but a moment later her foot slipped on a patch of algae, sending her forward. She slid into the deeper water with a shriek and landed in water that came up to her waist. She gasped a few times before shrieking out, "C–c–cold!"

Josie tried not to laugh, but before she could get control her foot hit the same algae patch, and she slid forward with the same results. The word "cold" didn't even come close to covering the sensation of the icy spring water as it slid up over her body. "H–how d–do the k–kids s–stand this? Th–this could th–throw a person into sh–shock!"

"Start moving around. Your body will heat back up in a moment." Caleb moved farther out into the water, allowing them more room to acclimate.

Sailor had already dropped into the deeper area and headed for her friends.

Caleb treaded water. "I'll stay nearby. You'll be fine."

They were isolated in their own little world by a small outcropping of rocks.

"No one can see you. C'mon. Give it a try. I'll be right here if you need me, but I'm guessing you won't."

Josie did as he asked and slowly moved out into the open water where she could no longer touch. He was right. Now that she was moving, the water didn't feel so icy cold. Either that or she was so numb she no longer had any feeling left in her limbs. She began treading water. "I can't believe I'm saying this, but it *is* refreshing."

"Yep." Caleb glanced over his shoulder. "Do you feel confident enough to swim to the other side? This is the kind of area we scoot the teens out of — though I have to admit, I like being over here with you." He waggled his eyebrows. "But I'm trying to set a good example."

"Caleb!" If he was trying to make her blush, it was working. She dove into the spring and started for the other side. He swam along beside her. She felt encouraged at his nearness, knowing he'd come to her aid if anything happened. She swam most of the way across underwater, eyes open, enjoying the clarity of the brisk water. Just as she reached the far side, there was a muffled splash, and a heavy object pushed her farther under the water. She panicked and took in a mouthful of water.

Strong hands pulled her upward. She burst through the surface of the water. She coughed and tried to catch her breath. "Caleb."

"I'm right here. Are you okay?" His strong arm supported her. His body was strong and solid against hers.

She found her footing on the ledge and tried to stand. Her legs were wobbly.

"Take your time. Catch your breath." Caleb surveyed her with concerned eyes. "You okay?"

"I'm so sorry, Miss Alvarez. I didn't see you there." One of the high-school boys stood in the water nearby, looking worried. Water cascaded down his face.

His friend sloshed over to join them. "I pushed him. I didn't see you, either. I'm really sorry. Are you okay?"

"I'm fine." She forced a smile then realized she really was fine. She'd survived being pushed underwater, no worse the wear. "I'm okay. You two go ahead and have fun — just watch out before you push next time — make sure the coast is clear."

They nodded and hurried away to another, less-populated area.

"Are you sure you're okay?" Caleb didn't seem to be in any hurry to remove his hand from her arm. "Those guys are pretty big."

"I'm fine. You were right there, just as you said you'd be."

"It took me a second to realize what happened. I'm sorry I wasn't faster to respond."

She laughed. "You couldn't have been any faster! He came at me like a brick wall. You were there before he'd even started back up again."

"All the same, I feel bad that you were hurt or scared on my watch. I know how you feel about the water. I wanted to make sure this was a pleasant experience for you. I should have made sure the area was clear before I led you over."

"If I remember correctly, I dove under the water and swam over here of my own accord." If he only knew how pleasant the feel of his arms were as they pulled her safely against his chest, he wouldn't be worried about her at all, but she wasn't about to tell him that. "I actually think it was a good experience. It showed me that even when something happens in the water, I can overcome it and feel safe."

"You're sure. You don't hurt anywhere?"

"I'm fine, Caleb. You've helped me reach a breakthrough. I was afraid, and you helped me face those fears. I think I can say with confidence I can pretty much face any water now, and I won't panic."

Caleb bobbed beside her. "Even if you fall off a cruise ship into rough water?"

"Even if I fall off a cruise ship in rough water. If I do, I'll use my skills. You've taught me well."

He grinned. "Your skills?"

"Yep. I'll tread water — like this." She moved forward into deeper water and showed him.

He nodded, and his smile lightened her heart.

"What if your puppy falls in the lake in the dark?"

"I don't have a puppy."

"Yet. It's figurative. Think abstract."

"If my theoretical puppy falls into the lake

at night, I'll jump in and save him."

"Fully clothed?"

"Fully clothed."

"Wet clothes can weigh you down."

"I'll take that into consideration and swim harder."

He studied her. "I do believe you're right. You're cured of your fear of water."

"Now I want to do the same for others. Help them face their fears." She looked past him, still treading water. "I want to help the girls at the clinic confront their biggest obstacles and help them see the potential they have to help others. I want them to see that they can make something of themselves, baby in tow or not."

"I like that. I think you'll succeed, too. I think whatever you put your mind to you can do it. I've seen you do just that already."

"Thanks, Caleb." She hoped he was right. More than ever she wanted to get home and have the chance to love on Mandy — to make up for her own impatience and emotional distance while working with her. Again she asked God to forgive her. He'd given her a job to do, and she'd failed in Mandy's case. As soon as she got home, she'd find Mandy and make things better.

Caleb watched her. "You sure you're okay? I think I just lost you there."

"I'm fine. I just realized God has given me some wonderful chances here in Lullaby, and I've already botched one terribly. I need to make things right."

Caleb reached over and pushed a wet strand of hair out of her eyes. "I can't imagine you doing anything to purposely hurt someone. You're being too hard on yourself."

"No, unfortunately I'm not. One of the girls — I can't be more specific — has had a really hard time of it, and instead of reaching out to her, I've resented her for the position she's put herself in."

"Resented her how?"

She wondered how much she should share.

"For years I've wanted to settle down and have a family. Marry a nice man. Have a few babies of my own. But for whatever reason, it's never happened." She blushed. "But these girls, they sometimes seem so callous about being pregnant. They don't seem to even appreciate the gift they've been given."

"Well," Caleb drawled softly, "you have to admit, they aren't having a baby in the best of circumstances. They don't have husbands or jobs or homes of their own. They've done things out of order. Their lives are at rock bottom."

"I know that — I've always known that — but still I've resented that they have this little one coming, and they don't even seem to care. I need to get back and fix things."

"We'll have you back in due time. For now, relax and have fun. I'm sure once you get back home, things will fall into place there, too. I think reaching your goal of ending your fear of water will help you when it comes to helping these girls face their fear of impending motherhood."

"You're wise beyond your years, Caleb. Thanks for understanding and for not judging me."

"Hey, I'm the last person to judge someone else. I'm about as far from perfect as a person can get. But I figure if God can call and use someone like me, He'll do great works through a person as sweet as you."

Not knowing what to say to such a great compliment, she avoided it and ducked underwater and swam away. She hoped he was right — that she could live up to his expectations — but in the meantime, just knowing he had such confidence in her gave her own confidence a boost.

NINE

Josie loved working her shift at the candy shop, but today, the first weekday home after they'd returned from the float trip, she found herself watching the clock, waiting for the shift to be over so she could go to the clinic and talk to Mandy.

Caleb walked out of his office and leaned on the counter. His untucked button-down shirt hung casually over his distressed jeans. His royal-blue shirt brought out the vivid blue of his eyes. "Got a big date?"

"What?" Josie dragged her eyes away and glanced back up at the big white clock hanging over the opening to the hall. "Oh. I'm sorry. No big date, but I can't wait to get to work so I can talk to — my client. She's one of my first appointments this afternoon. I'm thinking if I get over there soon enough, I can talk to her before she sees Cameron."

"Ah. The mystery girl." He stared at her, his expression unreadable. "Listen, we're slow this afternoon anyway. Why don't you go on over and see if she's there? I'll hold down the fort here at the shop."

"Are you sure? I know you're already shorthanded. Is Sailor feeling any better?"

"I think she's just tired from the trip. A good night's sleep and she'll be back to normal. And yes, I'm sure I can handle things. I don't think we'll have any huge bursts of business on an afternoon like this. They've called for rain to start up soon. If it rains, we'll be done for the day."

"If you're sure . . ." Josie was already untying her apron and pulling it over her head.

Caleb snagged it from her hands and motioned her to the door. "Go on. Talk to the girl. I'll be praying she's receptive to what you have to say. This'll give me some much-needed time to catch up on inventory and organize a bit. We've been so swamped I've let things slide back here. The prep room could use some attention."

Josie surveyed the neat room and raised her eyebrows. "You're saying this is messy?"

He shrugged. "It is to me."

"I see." Josie had a feeling he was making excuses so she'd leave without feeling guilty for abandoning him mid-shift. "I can come in early tomorrow or stay late to make up for this."

"No need. Now get over there, and take care of business!"

Josie did as he said. She entered the clinic and scanned the teens in the waiting area. There was no sign of Mandy, but the afternoon was still young. Mandy might not have shown up yet, or she might already be back with Cameron. Josie waved at Brit as she passed by the reception desk. They were all taking turns covering the front when they didn't have volunteers. Most of the time women from church came over to help run things, but when there was a scheduling gap, Brit, Cam, and Josie took turns as needed.

Cam was coming up the hall, escorting another teen to the waiting area as Josie passed by.

Josie waited until the teen walked out into the main area. "Hey, Cam. Has Mandy come by today?"

Cameron frowned. "I haven't seen her yet, but Brit hasn't mentioned her calling in to cancel, so I assume she'll be here soon."

"Good. I want to be sure I get a chance to talk to her."

She went into her office and called for her first client. The afternoon wore on with no sign of Mandy.

During a lull, Josie popped her head

around the corner into the reception area. "Brit, did Mandy ever call to cancel her appointment?"

"Not while I've been here. Mabel was in the office this morning, but I don't see any notes from her saying anyone canceled." Brit flipped through a small pile of yellow notes as she spoke.

Josie frowned. "All right. If she calls, could you please let me know?"

"Sure. I know she's missed a few appointments in the past. Is everything okay?"

"I hope so. Since she has missed several of her appointments, I was hoping she'd show today. She's seven months along and really needs to be here."

"She might still come in. Maybe she's having trouble finding a ride. I can have Matt track her down if you want me to."

"No, I don't want to scare her away. We'll see if she comes in late. If she doesn't, I'll figure out what to do later." She thanked Brit and returned to her office.

Josie's last scheduled appointment came and went with no sign of Mandy. She hoped everything was okay with the girl, but she had a sinking feeling that something was wrong.

Cameron popped her head around the doorway. "I'm leaving to head back to the inn. No word from Mandy?"

"Brit said she never called. I'm worried."

"I am, too. She needs prenatal care, and I know she needs moral support. Talking to you is important for her, whether she realizes it or not."

"I think I'll try to track her down."

"Want me to tag along?"

"No. She'll probably be annoyed enough at me for showing up. No reason to make her upset with both of us."

Cameron smiled. "True. You go play bad cop, and I'll be good cop next time she comes in."

"Gee thanks." Josie laughed. "I sure hope there is a next time. Maybe she's skipped town or something."

"She doesn't have the resources to go far. Let me know what you find out. I'll be praying."

"Thanks. I'll call you." Josie grabbed up her purse and headed out the door. Her car was parked on the far side of Caleb's shop.

He waved her down as she hurried past. "How'd it go? Did you get everything settled with your mystery girl?"

"No, she didn't show."

Concern etched his features. "I'm sorry to hear that. I know it was important to you that you talk to her. I prayed she'd show first thing this afternoon."

"I know. But she didn't. We had such a great time on the float trip, I'd expected to start the new week with a bang. I need to find her and make things right."

"So what's the next step? Will you just wait until she shows up?"

"No, actually I'm on my way to track her down now. I have a few different addresses that she's used here in the file. She moves around a lot."

"If you don't mind, I'd like to tag along."

"You might scare her off."

"I doubt it, but I think we should take that chance. You don't know the people around here or the area like I do. Most folks are friendly, but some don't take kindly to people snooping around. And trust me, if you're asking around about their kin, especially if she doesn't want to be found, they'll see it as snooping."

"Oh." Josie weighed her options. She could sit it out and wait, not invade Mandy's personal space, or she could take the chance of offending her and try to track her down. Since she felt she'd already offended her for the most part, she chose the second option. Her mother always said she wore her heart on her sleeve. If Mandy felt Josie's frustration or impatience, Josie needed to reach out and make up for it. She felt she had nothing to lose and everything to gain.

"I'll accept your escort."

"Let me tell Sailor, and I'll lock up the shop." He handed her his truck keys. "I'll drive. I don't think your car will handle some of the rougher terrain outside of town. I'll be right out, but if you don't mind, you can start the truck and turn on the air conditioner. From the looks of those clouds, the downpour's going to start any minute."

"I can do that." She reached out to take the keys, but just before she grabbed them she said, "Caleb, I appreciate the offer. I didn't relish the thought of going out to some of these addresses alone."

"I'll feel better going along. It's not a problem. I'll be right back." He hurried inside, and she walked over to climb into his truck.

"It's like she's fallen off the edge of the earth." Josie's discouragement was tangible. She ran her fingers through her hair and pulled it up on top of her head, only to let it fall back down around her neck as she mussed it and growled with frustration. "I really thought we'd find her by now. It's a small town."

"We have one more address to check out.

Don't give up yet."

A slight drizzle started, a prelude to the coming storm. Caleb turned onto a virtually nonexistent dirt path that led into the dense Ozark forest. Trees closed in on both sides of the truck, and Josie cringed as the branches scraped the roof and sides.

"This has to be wonderful for your paint job."

"What paint job?" He snickered. "Have you ever really *looked* at my truck? Don't worry about it. This is why I prefer older used vehicles to newer ones. They can go anywhere, and I don't have to worry about it. These woods and the rutted dirt roads are definitely hard on a vehicle. That's why I suggested we take mine, not yours."

"If you're sure — but if you'd rather, I could walk the rest of the way to the cabin. I don't mind."

"I mind. As soon as those clouds let loose, this dirt road will turn to a muddy river. Driving through it in a four-wheel-drive truck will be much easier than splashing through it on foot, trust me."

The road twisted and turned until Josie was thoroughly lost as to which direction they were heading.

"I would have never made it on foot. How far in do these people live?"

"These roads wind all over the mountains."

"How on earth do you know where to go?"

"I've been up here before. I'm guessing your mystery girl is one of my former youth group members."

"That would make sense. Her family is probably tied to the church one way or another since she knew about the clinic. So far most of our clients find us by word of mouth — a grandma, sister, or aunt goes to our church and tells them about the program."

"I know you have client confidentiality, but it isn't like I don't see which girls come and go at the clinic. Based on this address, we're looking for Mandy, right?"

Josie sighed. "Yes."

"I thought so. Her sister, Gina, was in my youth group. They lived up here with their grandmother until she passed away a year or so ago. Now Gina lives here with Mandy, or at least she did last I knew. Gina turned her back on church after her grandmother died."

"That's too bad. Most people turn to their church friends and hold on to those beliefs when they lose someone." She sighed. "So if I'd confided earlier who we were looking for, we could have found her by now?"

"Not necessarily. I've heard Gina is going through some hard times, and she and Mandy are at odds to say the least. Both girls inherited the house equally, but Gina's using her advantage of being older to cut Mandy out of their grandmother's will."

"That's terrible. Why would she do that? How do you know this stuff?"

"Her grandma's friend still attends the church. She's come in to talk to me about it a few times, to get advice. Since we're both working with the same girls, I can share with you. She's tried to help but says Gina's boyfriend has moved in, and it hasn't been easy for Mandy. She thinks they — or at least the boyfriend — might be cooking drugs out here. That's why I insisted I come along. I was afraid you'd run into something like this. Not specifically with Mandy, but with whoever it was you were chasing down."

"I feel worse than ever. I'm supposed to listen and help guide these girls, and I had no clue how hard things were for her."

"Don't feel bad. How could you know? Mandy is a hard nut to crack, even in the best of circumstances. Now that she's lost her grandmother, her sister has turned on her, and the boyfriend never wants her around — she's shut down. It's a hard life out here in the hills. The people are proud and don't like to accept help even when it's offered. But even with all that, I think we can reach Mandy if we can get her out of this situation and into a safe place like the center. She has a good head on her shoulders. Right now she has to grieve her grandmother's passing and deal with the unexpected pregnancy. She has to fight for her right to live in her own house. Any one of those things would put most people into depression. She's been bombarded by them."

"I know. I'll make it right for her if I have the chance. Is it safe to go to the house?"

"We'll announce ourselves and keep our distance."

Josie had dealt with enough similar problems in her practice back home to understand the dynamics, but she'd never seen the clients outside her office walls. This experience was giving her much-needed field input into the lives of the people she counseled. She was glad to have Caleb at her side as she navigated these uncharted waters.

A log cabin came into view. The large covered porch gave it a homey atmosphere. "I'd have never guessed."

"What? That this could be a drug house?

Mandy's grandma would roll over in her grave if she knew. You can't be too careful around here, even if things look good from the outside. If you don't know an area or a family, it's best to proceed with caution or find someone who knows the family to go along with you. Like me." He grinned.

"I have a lot to learn." Again she counted her blessings and was glad that Caleb was in her life.

He pulled the truck into the clearing and honked the horn.

"You sit tight."

Josie nodded, more than happy to obey.

He opened the door and stepped out to place one leg on the running board while he waited for a response. He looked ready to duck back into the truck on a moment's notice. He didn't have to wait long.

The door opened a crack, and the end of a rifle pushed through the opening. A moment later an older version of Mandy stepped out onto the porch. "Pastor Caleb? What're you doin' up here?"

"Hey, Gina. How are you?"

"I'm doin' fine, but my boyfriend won't be too fond of drivin' in to see a man on the premises."

"I thought this was your and Mandy's place. Do I need to clarify that for your boyfriend?"

"Not if you want to drive outta here alive. He's got a mean temper." She glanced around, nervousness rolling off her skin.

"Then I'll state my business and be on my way. I'm looking for Mandy. I have a friend here who wants to make sure she's okay."

"Mandy don't live here no more." Gina lowered the rifle and walked over to lean on the railing. "She and Frank don't get along. Frank finally sent her packin'."

"Do you think that's fair, Gina? This is Mandy's home, too."

"Not anymore. She was disrespectful to Frank, and that's that. He don't tolerate no backtalk, and she couldn't learn to keep her mouth shut."

"Can you give me an address where we can find her?"

"No. Last I knew she'd worn out her welcome everywhere she'd gone. Good riddance is all I can say."

Josie felt sick. She'd seen the pretty side of Lullaby and hadn't thought about this other side.

Caleb said his good-byes and lowered himself into the cab. He turned the truck around and started back down the path. When he glanced over at her, his blue eyes reflected her concern. "We'll find her, Josie."

"I hope so. More than ever now that I've seen how alone she is." Josie's nerves were shot. She hoped they'd get out of the woods before they passed Frank coming in — not that there was any room to pass. He didn't sound like anyone she wanted to meet. "What if something happened to her? I'll feel so awful. I could have been the one to help her."

"Did you try? Yes. I know you well enough to know that you did. Mandy has a hard life and doesn't open up to anyone. She crawled in her shell when her granny died and hasn't been the same since. Next thing I knew she showed up pregnant, and I wouldn't be surprised if the baby doesn't belong to her sister's boyfriend."

"That's a terrible thing to even think about!"

"It is. So in that way, it's a good thing that Mandy isn't there anymore. If he hasn't already hurt her, he would have in due time."

"What if he did hurt her?"

"It's a possibility, but I don't think even Gina would allow him to get by with that. Besides, we don't know anything for sure."

"What if he hurt Mandy and Gina didn't know?"

"Gina's not stupid. She'd know."

"What do we do now?"

"We pray for guidance and see where God leads us."

They pulled out on the main road, and Caleb headed down the mountain toward town. A few miles down they passed a small roadside park. Josie motioned toward it. "Can we stop there? It looks like as good as any place to pray."

The rain had stopped for the moment, and she longed for a breath of fresh air. She wanted the rain-kissed air to rinse the images of Mandy, alone and fighting Gina's overbearing boyfriend, out of her head.

Caleb swung into the parking lot. They walked over to the lone picnic table and sat side by side on top of it. They stared out over the rolling hills. Caleb held out his strong hand, and Josie gladly joined it with her smaller one. She felt a tingle at the connection and settled close against his side. His strong presence gave her courage. Caleb bowed his head.

"Dear Lord, we come to You in prayer to ask for Your guidance in finding Mandy. We pray for her safety and protection as we search for her. Please let her know she has people who care about her and have her come back to us. Help her to accept our love and concern when we do find her. Give Josie peace and discernment on how to help Mandy's hurting heart. In Your name, Amen."

"That was beautiful." Josie wiped an errant tear from her eye. She glanced around the pretty park. "It's so peaceful here. Who would know that people like Gina and Frank live right around the curve? I wish we could help Gina, too."

"I know." Caleb held tight to her hand. "But like I said, some people don't want help even when it's offered. Gina knew she had us to turn to and chose not to. Instead she fell in with Frank and cut Mandy out of her life. She's hardened her heart. We can pray she finds her way back, but until she makes that decision for herself, she has to deal with the consequences."

Josie nodded, understanding but not liking it. She pointed over to a small path. "Where does that lead?"

"There's a small stream and a pretty covered bridge that runs over it. Since the storm's holding off, do you want to walk over and see it?"

"Might as well while we're here." She felt guilty that they were sightseeing while Mandy was missing, but she figured they'd done all they could for one day. She had no more addresses to follow up with. Caleb tugged her down from the tabletop. She stood on the bench and jumped to the ground. "Guess it's a good thing we wore our walking shoes."

"I would have had you go back and change if you hadn't. As you've seen, the paths — even to people's front doors — aren't always easy to navigate."

"Mandy's aunt's porch wasn't easy to navigate, and it was close to town!"

"Hmm. That's true. Thanks."

"For what?"

"You've just given me an idea."

"What kind of idea?" They meandered down the path, neither seeming to care that small raindrops had begun to fall.

"I've been trying to come up with some youth group plans for the fall. Why don't we plan a youth activity that centers around fixing up the houses of those in need? We can paint, do repairs — we'll get professionals to volunteer to oversee that type of thing — we can even clean up the yards and mow lawns."

"I think that's a wonderful idea! It'll be perfect come fall, too. We have the amusement park trip in a couple of weeks, right? Then we have nothing planned from there. Maybe we can plan our first workday early in September."

Caleb grinned down at her. "We'll bring it up at the next meeting."

The path turned, and the scene before them turned surreal. A wide stream gurgled down the hill. The fast-moving water tumbled across boulders and logs. Mist rose from the stream, enveloping the underside of the covered bridge in a wispy haze. Dark clouds loomed over the green hills and threatened a cloud burst that they'd be caught in if they didn't hurry back to the truck.

But even with the storm looming, Josie felt drawn to the area. "It's so pretty. I'd love to come back with my camera."

"I know. Takes you back in time, doesn't it?"

"Yes. Why is it out here in the middle of nowhere?"

"The bridge used to lead to a town just over that next hill. The town died out around the turn of the century, and the bridge fell out of use. The new road into Lullaby was built, and no one used the road to the bridge anymore. Now you can't even find the original road. It's hidden in the overgrowth."

A clap of thunder announced the storm's arrival, and Caleb tugged her hand. "We'll ride it out in the bridge. If we're lucky it'll blow over quickly. We'll head home after it passes."

They ran into the covered bridge just as a huge bolt of lightning lit up the sky. Josie screamed and ducked inside. In the momentary flash of light, she realized they weren't alone.

TEN

"Don't come any closer, and I won't hurt you."

Caleb could hear the fear in the shaky voice. The lightning flash had come and gone, but not before Caleb saw the end of a shotgun pointed their way. He couldn't tell if the gun was real or not, but he wasn't going to take a chance. "We're not here to hurt you. We're just trying to ride out the storm. We didn't know anyone would be in here."

"Mandy?" Josie called out and shifted beside him. She placed a hand on Caleb's arm. The rain pounded down on the bridge's roof, drowning out their voices. So Josie stood on her tiptoes and leaned close to his ear when she spoke. "Caleb — I think God led us to Mandy."

A wisp of her intoxicating floral perfume floated his way on the breeze. He forced his thoughts back to the woman with the gun. Josie seemed sure it was Mandy. Caleb's

171

anxiety decreased a few notches. He hadn't relished the thought of climbing back up the path in the storm, but if an unknown person held a rifle pointed in their direction, they'd be smart to move on. If the gun-toting female was Mandy, they'd likely be safe. At least she knew them.

"Who are you?" the shaky voice called across the darkness.

Or she'd know them once they introduced themselves.

"It's me, Josie, from the clinic in town. Caleb, the youth leader from church, is with me. We've been looking for you all day."

"You been lookin' for me?" She sounded incredulous. "How'd you know I was here?"

"Is this a weird coincidence, Caleb?" Josie whispered, once again framing him in her perfume.

"I don't believe in coincidences." He shook his head, even though he knew she couldn't see him. "I think we can safely say God had a firm part in this one."

"I agree." Josie's soft laugh carried across the inches separating them. "In all honesty, Mandy, I think God led us to you. We went to your grandmother's after trying the other addresses in your file. I was worried when you didn't show up for your appointment. We pulled over here to pray. You're getting close enough to your due date that you really should be checked by Cameron on a regular basis from here on out, and I wanted to make sure everything was okay."

"I didn't exactly have a ride."

"You do now."

"Right. And you're gonna bring me all the way back up here?"

"I will if I need to, but I'd like to discuss some other options with you. Can we come over there?"

Caleb figured Josie had seen the same thing he had during subsequent lightning flashes. A sleeping bag lay rolled out next to a garbage bag full of clothes. A lantern lay on the ground beside it. They heard Mandy moving around. Light flickered from the lantern. Caleb felt sick to his stomach. He couldn't even think about Sailor living in such conditions. No teen should be without love and protection and support.

"I try to conserve battery power." She pushed her stringy hair back from her forehead.

Caleb noticed a hint of a bruise near her eye. Someone had knocked her around.

Josie hurried forward. "Oh, Mandy. You've been living all the way out here all alone?"

Mandy did her customary shrug. "I like being alone."

"Sweetheart, no one likes being this alone."

"It beats having Frank breathin' down my neck."

"I can imagine." Josie stepped closer to Mandy. "Did he — did he hurt you?"

Mandy looked down at her stomach. "Not in the way you're thinkin', no, but he hurt me plenty enough in other ways. I'd rather live alone here ten times over than to ever look that snake in the eyes again."

"Is he the one who put that bruise on your face? He shouldn't be allowed to get by with beating on anyone, let alone a pregnant teen." Caleb wanted to go back and throttle the guy.

Mandy's eyes widened. "You can't go after him. He'll take it out on Gina."

Gina — the sister who allowed Mandy to be kicked out of her own home. That lone comment allowed Caleb a glimpse into Mandy's heart, and he saw her potential. He'd tuck that thought away, and one day he'd share it with her. He felt sure that one day soon Mandy would feel safe enough to hear praise and encouragement from him.

Josie raised the heel of her hand to her forehead. "I can see I have a lot more questions I need to ask my girls from now on. Mandy, will you consider coming back with me to the center? Several of the rooms are ready and just waiting for someone like you. You can have your pick. I'd love to have you there with me. I thought I'd like living alone, too, but I miss having my sisters around. It's far too quiet, and I'd love some company."

A flicker of hope lit Mandy's eyes, but she didn't speak or move.

Josie kept her voice casual as she continued. "I couldn't wait to settle in my suite, but now I rattle around in the place and wonder why I ever dreamed of being alone. It isn't what it's cracked up to be in my experience. I'd love to have you join me."

"I'd have my own room?"

"You'll have your own room, yes. It's fully furnished with a bed, a dresser, and a crib. There's a rocking chair and a changing table. We have everything you'll need for the baby, should you choose to keep him or her. Three square meals a day and all the snacks you want. The rooms are already decorated, but you can pick your comforter and linens from the new stash we have waiting. What do you say?"

"I've never had anything like that before." Mandy licked her lips. "And I haven't eaten all day. The food sounds downright enticin'."

"Oh, Mandy. Let's get you home and get some food in that belly. You have a baby in there trying to grow."

"Don't I know it?" Mandy rubbed her hand over her stomach. "Even when I do have access to food it seems I'm hungry all the time."

Caleb stepped forward. "The storm's moving away. Let's get out of here while we have a chance. The path will be slippery as it is, so let's take as little as possible with us for now. I can always come back for the rest of your things when the weather clears. I'd like to get to the truck before the next cloud burst hits."

Josie looked around at the items scattered around on the floor. "What do you need to take right now? Do you have any valuables?"

"Not hardly. I don't really need anythin' here other than some clothes to change into." She kicked the items around with her foot. "Everything's pretty dirty though. That's another reason I didn't want to come to the clinic today, even if I'd had a ride. I always look like a mess compared to the others there."

"No one would have cared what you looked like, Mandy. If you want to grab some clothes, we do have a washer and dryer. But we also have some cute maternity clothes stored away that you can go through. They're clean and stylish and just waiting for the right person to come along and use them. You're welcome to take what you need."

"Then I guess we're ready to go." Mandy's voice was weary. "None of this stuff is worth keeping."

"I'll come back to clean it up tomorrow. Do you want me to pitch it all? I can bring it back, and you could go through it if you'd like." Caleb could carry everything out in one load. Mandy didn't own much, and the poor kid was willing to walk away from what little she did have. Again he couldn't help but compare her lack to Sailor's excess. It might do Sailor some good to come up and see how Mandy was living.

Caleb watched Josie smile with anticipation. She was in her prime. "Let's get her back to the center so I can help her clean up, pick fresh clothes, feed her, and get her settled into her room. This storm isn't a good place for any of us. I think we'll all appreciate getting somewhere warm and dry."

Josie's smile lit the dim area. How she could ever think she'd been cold to the teen was beyond Caleb's understanding. She had a natural empathy and compassion that wouldn't be mistaken as impatience.

Mandy bloomed during the ride home. She opened up under Josie and Caleb's gentle nudging and concern, and she shared some of her recent experiences that had led to her living in the bridge. Josie cringed to think what would have happened if Mandy had had a medical emergency while living in such conditions. And what would have happened when winter came?

Josie didn't give voice to her troubled thoughts. Instead, she watched as a sense of peace fell over Mandy as they drove toward town. They drove home in another downpour. All three were crowded into the cab of Caleb's truck, and Mandy actually laughed as they ran from Caleb's truck to the center's front door. Even though he dropped them off a few feet from the entrance — as close as he could get — they were drenched by the time Josie managed to unlock the door.

"Come over for dinner. We'll celebrate," Caleb yelled as they tumbled through the door.

"What are we celebrating?" Josie hollered back.

"Mandy, of course." He grinned. "Finding her calls for some serious celebrating, don't you think?"

Josie turned to Mandy and could have sworn tears were coursing down the teen's cheeks. It was hard to tell for sure with all the rainwater cascading down her face. "Is that okay with you? You know Sailor, right?"

"No one's ever celebrated me before."

"Well, it's high time that changed." She turned to Caleb. "We'll be there. Seven o'clock okay?"

"Seven will be fine. See you then." He drove off with a splash of tires.

"I like him," Mandy stated.

"Me, too," Josie agreed.

They shared a conspiratorial smile.

"What now?" Mandy looked lost in the large open room.

"First off, we need to get you into dry clothes. The last thing you need is to get sick. I'll show you the bathroom, and you can shower while I find you something to wear. Later we'll go through the items we've accumulated, and you can pick out the clothes you prefer."

"Sounds nice." Mandy looked years younger. She relaxed her hard shell and allowed Josie a glimpse of the softer person inside.

They headed upstairs, and Josie showed Mandy the finished rooms. Mandy picked the one closest to Josie's suite. The room had an old-fashioned flare with delicate pink and off-white wallpaper and an antique doll décor.

"This reminds me of my granny." Mandy caressed the pretty wallpaper.

"This room's one of my favorites, too. The bathroom is over here." Josie motioned to the connecting door. "You'll eventually have to share it with one other girl, but for now, it's all yours."

"This is so nice. I don't know what to say."

"You don't have to say anything, Mandy. I wish I'd done a better job at reaching out to you before. I'm sorry I didn't make you feel welcome or safe enough to open up about how bad things really were."

Mandy's eyes registered surprise. "Why would you say that? I've always felt welcome here. I just hate comin' in dirty or late. I'm always a mess. I figured you were judging me because you always seem to have everything together, and you always look so pretty. You dress nice."

Lesson learned. Josie hadn't thought about how she'd come across to the teens. She dressed as she always had when going to her counseling practice in Texas. First chance she had, she'd go shopping for some clothes that were comfortable and would put the girls at ease.

She started to say she hadn't judged Mandy based on her clothing or anything else, but could she truly state that? She'd felt frustrated when Mandy came in looking rough. She'd thought the teen just didn't care. She'd never given consideration to the hardships Mandy had to overcome just to get to the clinic for her appointments.

While Josie and Cameron were focused on fetal nutrition and a healthy pregnancy, Mandy was struggling to survive.

"I'm sorry I made you feel that way. That was never my intent. Can we start fresh? I think I can learn a lot from you, too."

Mandy frowned. "Sure. But I don't think I have anything to teach you."

Josie laid a hand on Mandy's arm. "Believe me, you've already taught me more than you'll ever know."

She pointed Mandy in the direction of the hall closet where she'd stashed the toiletry donations. Mandy picked out what she needed for her shower while Josie went to the storage room to pick up a towel and some clothes.

One hour later, Caleb met them at their back door with a huge umbrella in hand.

"I wasn't sure you had an umbrella. I

didn't think you'd want a repeat of earlier."

"You've got that right." Josie ducked under the protective cover and motioned Mandy to join them. She hugged her close so she wouldn't get wet. The wind had died down, and they walked slowly toward Caleb's home with the rain gently pelting against the top of the umbrella.

"Sailor doesn't mind my comin' over, does she?" Mandy hugged her arms around her middle. "I don't want to invade or interfere with your family time. I don't want to impose."

"You're not imposing at all. The more the merrier we always say. In fact, she's happily manning the stove while I'm escorting you." Caleb opened his back door and motioned for them to go in. After he finished battling the umbrella closed, they climbed the steps from the back entry to his home on the second floor. The spicy scent of spaghetti and garlic drifted their way.

"My mouth is watering." Josie closed her eyes and inhaled.

"Mine, too." Mandy followed suit.

Caleb stared at them. "Uh oh, I didn't think to ask if the garlic or spices would upset Mandy's stomach. It's been awhile since I've had to think about these things."

Mandy shrugged. "Nothing seems to

bother me. Dinner smells delicious. I promise I'll enjoy every bite."

"Good deal." He released his breath and led them into the kitchen. "Sit. Relax. Sailor and I will serve up the food."

Josie sank happily into a chair. The long day had ended well, but the stress of Josie's emotions pulled at her, making her feel weary. "Sailor, did your dad tell you his ideas about the youth group serving some of the area's residents this fall?"

"No." Sailor paused at the stove. "You mean serve like this? We're going to feed people?"

Caleb laughed. "No, but that's what Josie made it sound like. Maybe we should work a few meals in, too."

"I know lots of people who would appreciate a warm meal," Mandy interjected. Her new clothes seemed to give her a newfound confidence. "A lot of my *former* neighbors" — she slanted Josie a smile — "would appreciate it. I'd love to help with that."

"I like the idea, too." Josie loved the way a natural camaraderie was developing in the small kitchen. "I think we need to consider it. But, Sailor, your dad's idea was more of a physical serving. We'd go out into the community and help clean up yards, mow for those who are sick or too weak or who have husbands in the military. We can paint, put plastic over windows to help hold the heat in when cold weather hits — that type of thing."

"Sounds fun." Sailor shrugged. "I'm in."

"Me, too," Mandy quipped. She glanced down at her expanding belly. "At least as much as I can help in this condition."

Josie patted her hand. "We'll find things for you to do, too. Even if you can't do physical labor, you can sit and visit with the residents. I'm sure they'd love to have someone sit down and talk to them."

"I think I'd be good at that."

"I know you will be." Josie figured she would — since Mandy had just experienced the same type of situation.

"So, Mandy, speaking of youth, now that you're here, are you going on the next youth trip with us?" Sailor carried two plates over to the table and set one in front of Mandy and the other at the empty seat next to Mandy. Sailor settled into the chair. "It's going to be fun. You have to say yes."

Caleb brought two more plates of pasta for Josie and himself. He exchanged a glance with Josie as he set hers before her. She smiled up at him.

"Youth trip?" Mandy whipped her head up and looked from Caleb to Josie. "Um, I don't know anything about it."

"She has to come, right Daddy? If she's living with Josie now, she'll get to come along? We can't leave her behind."

Mandy nervously rubbed a thumb along the edge of the table. "I don't have money for a trip right now. I can stay at the center, though, even if Josie goes. I'll be fine."

"No, you have to come." Sailor again sent an imploring look in her father's direction. "We'll get the money for your portion. We're going to an amusement park in Branson. You'll love it."

Mandy laughed. "I can't ride any of the rides. It'd be a waste of money to drag me along."

With those words Josie's mind was made up. "Of course she's coming along. Having you along, Mandy, would never be a waste. You're coming with us, and that's that."

Sailor took a bite of her spaghetti and slurped the noodles in a way that had Caleb looking at her in exasperation.

She ignored him. "Seriously — they have all these shows, and the food is awesome. You can ride the train and several of the other rides even though you're pregnant. I'll hang out with you. We'll have fun."

Caleb slammed his hand down on the table, and they all jumped. "So it's decided!

Mandy's going along. She has no say in the subject — the family has spoken."

"See? Daddy says," Sailor chirped.

Mandy's forehead wrinkled with confusion, but her mouth tipped into a smile. "I guess I can go. Sounds like the decision has been made for me."

Josie made a face at him. They couldn't let Mandy think she had no say in her life, or she'd take off out of the center like a scared rabbit.

"What?" Caleb asked, all innocence.

Josie shook her head. "Ignore them, Mandy. They get goofy sometimes. You have full say in this matter and any other subject that pertains to you. If you want to go, you'll go. But if you don't want to go, we'll figure out an alternative." She placed her hand on Mandy's. "I do promise you, though, from what I've heard about this place, it's a wonderful place to visit whether you can physically handle the rides or not. But the decision is yours to make, not Caleb's or Sailor's or mine."

"But she agreed." Caleb spread his arms to his side, palms up.

"I did. If you all really don't mind, I'd like to go." Mandy looked as hopeful as a kid staring at a Christmas display in the front window of a toy store."

Josie sent Caleb a pointed look. "*Now* it's settled."

He rolled his eyes. "Women. Always have to be in control."

"When it comes to our own lives, yes, we ladies like to be in control. And you know that's the way it should be."

"Yes, ma'am. Of course I do." He glanced around the table. "And I'm smart enough to realize that since I'm sadly outnumbered here, I'd be crazy to say otherwise."

The conversation turned to school, church, and other topics, but Josie spent most of the time watching Mandy blossom under their love and attention. She smiled and twisted shiny brown hair around her finger as Caleb talked about his antics with Matt in high school. She placed her chin on her hand, and her green eyes sparkled as Sailor contributed her own antics from previous years. With her belly hidden under the table, Mandy looked like any other teen spending time with friends over dinner. Every once in a while she'd interject her thought or opinion on something the father-daughter duo had said. She acted as referee during their mock arguments, and Sailor and Caleb both acquiesced to her opinion. Sailor seemed to relax in Mandy's presence for the first time in weeks. Josie prayed the two could possibly become good friends.

When Mandy caught Josie staring, a radiant smile filled her thin face. Josie realized she'd been placing limitations on God, that perhaps He had a different plan when it came to surrounding her with kids and growing her a family. She'd been focused on a husband and a newborn baby, but just maybe, God planned to fill her desire for a family in a less traditional way.

ELEVEN

The weekend for the trip to the amusement park rolled around, and Josie couldn't help but notice that this time, when they arrived at the church to load into the vehicles, an unusually quiet Sailor climbed into the back of the SUV with Mandy.

"Everything okay?" Josie whispered as Sailor slipped past her.

Sailor nodded and sank into the far seat in the back corner. Mandy sat down beside her. Allie joined them a few minutes later. The middle-school boys, who beelined for the SUV, were redirected to the larger van, where Brian and his friends were already sitting.

Josie closed the car door and leaned against it. She turned to Cameron. "Are you sure it's okay for Mandy and Allie to come along? I mean, they're here and are coming no matter what, but the amusement part of the trip won't be too much for them, will it?"

"I'm sure they'll be fine. They're both about seven months along in their pregnancies. If they're careful about what they ride at the amusement park, they'll do fine. It doesn't hurt that they have their own personal nurse-midwife tagging along." She fluttered her hands down her length as she referred to herself and posed, grinning. "The heat can be an issue, but we'll go to the park after three today, so I'm not too worried about that. I'm more worried about them overheating and dehydrating in this heat if tomorrow is as hot as today. We'll need to watch and make sure they drink plenty of water. That's a concern for all the kids, by the way. But I'll keep an eye on the mommys-to-be. I'm sure they'll do fine." She glanced around at the milling teens. "If you don't mind, I think I'll ride in here with you so I can keep tabs on them starting now."

"And so you can avoid riding in the noisy vehicle with all the other teens?" Josie laughed. "I do believe we'll have the quieter ride."

Caleb had left all the seats in place for this trip. They'd decided to pull along a trailer for the luggage, which allowed more space for riders. Several extra people had decided to come along for the trip to Branson.

Josie counted heads. "I think everyone's here. I'm glad you and Seth signed on to help. We'd be short a few hands if you hadn't."

"I'm excited to see more of the area and to spend some time with the kids." Cameron's blue eyes sparkled. "Working with youth keeps a person young. I'm feeling much too old as it is."

Josie snorted. "Old my foot. You're younger than I am."

"I'm closing in on thirty and feeling every day of it," Cameron teased.

Caleb walked up and motioned for them to climb in. Seth appeared at Cameron's side and opened the door for her. Josie didn't miss the blush that colored her friend's cheeks. She couldn't help but think Seth would be a perfect match for Cameron. Seth walked around to the far side to climb in beside Cameron.

"Are you going to join us?" Caleb held the front passenger door open for Josie and waited for her to climb in.

"Sorry." She hurried to do so, relishing the cool air that blasted from the vents. She scooted her legs out of the way, and Caleb shut the door.

"So, Josie," Seth asked warmly from the backseat, "I figure it's a good sign that you survived the float trip and came back for more. Are you ready for this?"

Josie shifted in her seat so she could see him. "I'm as ready as I'll ever be. They're a fun group, but we're so glad you're coming along. I was just telling Cameron how much we appreciate the extra help."

"I'm more than happy to be here. I needed a break from the remodeling at the inn."

Caleb climbed in the driver's side and started the engine. Matt pulled the large van out of the church parking lot, and Caleb waited a moment and fell in behind him. Josie glanced back at Sailor, who was already listening to her iPod. Mandy appeared to be playing a game with Allie on Sailor's iPad.

Josie returned her attention to Seth. "How's the construction going? I miss the daily updates, though Cameron keeps me posted on the major things."

"It's coming together pretty well. We should be fully functioning in time for the holidays."

"That's great. I'm sure you're ready to get back to a normal operating schedule."

"I am, and I know Aunt Ginny's ready to cook for more guests. How do you like your new quarters?"

"I like them a lot better now that Mandy's there with me." She looked back at the girls.

Mandy glanced up and shared a smile with Josie before returning her attention to her game.

"As to my specific quarters, they're surprisingly similar to my suite at the inn. I feel right at home. Seems someone with a familiar style had some input on the design?"

"Guilty as charged. We figured whoever lived there would appreciate a cozy suite with a nice bath."

"My suite's nice, too," Mandy piped up from the backseat. "I've never stayed in such a wonderful place."

"Good," Seth replied. "Glad to hear it. That's exactly the response we intended and hoped for when we planned the layout of the second floor."

They fell into a comfortable silence as they drove around the winding mountain roads. Occasionally Josie would hear Mandy, Allie, and Sailor talking in the backseat as they exchanged an electronic device or discussed a song one or the other liked. Josie was glad to see that they were getting along.

Seth and Cameron carried on a quiet

conversation for the most part. Every so often Seth explained points of interest she and Josie might like to visit. Caleb added a comment here and there, but mostly he just drove, uncharacteristically silent like his daughter.

They pulled off at a rest stop, and everyone scattered.

Josie walked over to Caleb. "Is something wrong? You don't seem like yourself today."

"I'm fine. I'm just a bit tired I guess."

Josie hadn't ever seen him too tired to talk. Even after the float trip, he'd been his usual talkative self. Maybe he and Sailor had had a tiff before leaving home that morning.

"Want someone else to drive the rest of the way in? I don't mind, and I'm sure Seth would love to take the wheel."

"Nah, I'm fine. More brain weary than bone weary. I'm sure I'll feel better once we get settled at the hotel."

"You sure it isn't more than that?"

"I don't know. I'm kind of worried about Sailor. She's quieter than usual, and if you've noticed, she and Brian aren't talking."

"I did notice. She didn't say anything to you?"

"Not a word."

They dropped the topic as Seth and Cameron walked over to join them.

Seth leaned against the van. "What's today's agenda?"

"We'll get to town around lunchtime since we left midmorning. We can grab a bite to eat, find our hotel, and do an early check-in. The kids should be able to swim for a couple of hours before we head over to the amusement park," Caleb answered. "If we go to the amusement park after three, we get tomorrow free, so we'll spend the afternoon and early evening there then come back here for dinner, more swimming, and bedtime."

"Tomorrow we'll be at the park all day?"

"Yep. We'll leave the park again before dinner, order pizza, and eat at the pool. After they're good and worn out, we'll head for the various hotel rooms. Sunday morning we'll get up, have a small service together, pack up, check out, and head home. It's a tight trip, but we'll fit a lot in."

Cameron spent Friday afternoon watching out for Mandy and Allie. Sailor tagged along. She seemed to prefer the quiet of the small group.

Josie insisted on taking her turn hanging out with Sailor, Mandy, and Allie on Saturday. Cameron and Seth took their group of kids and headed in one direction as Matt and Brit took another group and went opposite. They tried to divide by ages and interests. The more adventurous kids went with Matt and Brit.

Caleb glanced at their motley crew. "We have middle-school boys who are full of energy, two expectant mothers, and Sailor, who can get sick just looking at rides that go in circles."

"Nice combination, don't you think?" Josie laughed. "Did Sailor get her queasiness from you?"

"No. I live for the wilder rides. She got that trait from her mother."

"I'm more than happy to stick to the more mellow rides, so it looks like you get the boys, and I'll take the girls." She whispered a silent prayer of thanks for the arrangement. She did not want to spend the long day with the middle-school boys. "We'll hit the shops and some of the shows while y'all spin yourselves crazy."

"We'll meet up with you in a couple of hours to eat and maybe watch some shows together — how's that sound?"

The younger boys groaned.

Josie thought it sounded really good. She hadn't spent any time with Caleb since they'd arrived the day before. He'd taken some of the older boys around the previous afternoon. She lowered her voice as they walked toward the split in the path. "Did you get a chance to talk to Brian yesterday?"

"Not really. He seems fine. He's goofing off with the other boys like he doesn't have a care in the world."

"Hmm. Typical. Well, maybe they just had a little fight. I'm sure they'll patch things up soon enough."

"I'm not sure I want them to."

"I know." She gave his arm a reassuring squeeze and hurried over to join the girls. She stepped between them and hooked arms with Allie and Mandy. Sailor fell in beside Allie. "Where shall we begin, ladies?"

"The roller coaster?" Mandy asked hopefully.

"Not a chance, little momma." Josie nudged the teen. "I think Cameron was pretty clear on what you could and couldn't do. What's plan B?"

"What would happen if she rode the roller coaster?" Sailor asked.

"I'm not a nurse — you'd be better off asking Cameron that question — but I'm sure Mandy could go into premature labor. The placenta could pull loose from the uterus. The baby would be shaken all around. None of it would be healthy or safe!"

"So what if I want to ride the roller coaster?" Sailor persisted.

"Um." Josie glanced around. Caleb and the boys were nowhere to be seen. "I guess if you want to do that, we'll have to find one of the other groups, and you can join them."

"You don't ride roller coasters?"

"I do, but I don't want to leave Mandy and Allie alone."

"We're not invalids!" Mandy laughed. "I don't mind sitting over there and waiting for you to get finished with the ride. Allie, what about you?" She pointed to a bench in the shade. "I was so tired yesterday I could hardly stand it. I want to pace myself better today."

"Sounds good to me," Allie agreed. "Take Sailor on her ride."

"Are you sure?" Josie didn't want to leave them. They were more than old enough to sit on a bench by themselves, but she didn't want them to feel like they were being left out. "I don't mind calling one of the other groups over to ride with you, Sailor, and I can sit here with Mandy and Allie."

Mandy sighed. "Josie, please! I appreciate the concern, but I'm perfectly able to sit on

198

a bench and wait while you ride a ride."

"I know, but —"

Allie waved her away. "No buts. We'll be fine. I'm so glad I was able to come along on this trip. It doesn't matter to me if I can ride all the rides or not. I have plenty of things here to keep me entertained. Look. I can hear that band that's playing up the hill. We can watch the little kids playing in the area across the way. We can watch the puppet show over there." She motioned to a small outdoor theater. "If we get hungry, we can go over and buy some kettle corn or something. You go have fun with Sailor."

"If you're both sure . . ."

"We are! Go! Sailor, get her out of here!" Mandy laughed.

They walked over to get in line for an indoor roller coaster. Josie perused Sailor. "You sure you're up to this? Your dad said you get sick if you ride the wrong thing."

"Having second thoughts about being my seatmate? Don't worry. I shouldn't get sick on a ride like this. It doesn't spin much, I'm sure."

"The sign says it isn't for pregnant mothers or people with heart conditions or back problems. It can't be all that tame."

"Can't be all that rough, either. Look at all the small children in line. If they can handle it, so can I."

"I'll trust your judgment." Josie couldn't help but think Sailor had some kind of agenda in wanting to ride the ride. "Does this have something to do with Brian?"

Sailor's mouth turned down at the edges. Her blue eyes grew hard. "No."

"Can I ask what happened between you two?"

"We had a fight."

"I kind of figured that." She waited, but Sailor didn't offer any more information. Josie didn't push. The lines of people twisted and turned back and forth, allowing no privacy for a talk of this nature. They stepped through the turnstile and fell into place in one of the numbered squares on the floor. The coaster rolled through the opening at the far end. The riders' hair stuck out in all directions, but they were smiling.

Sailor's eyes were hard and bitter, but her mouth formed a grim smile. "Ready? I am."

"Ready as I'll ever be," Josie quipped. She sat beside Sailor and pulled the lap bar toward them. She wasn't big on roller coasters, but this one looked fun. She wished she could share it with Caleb, though, instead of an angry teen.

The coaster jerked and slowly started

forward. They flew through a realistic-looking town that appeared to be on fire. Blasts of heat gave the illusion that the fire was real. The roller coaster twisted and turned through several scenarios before picking up speed toward a broken area of track. Just when it looked like the cars would go off the edge, they dropped downward and then twisted hard to the right, then to the left, only to splash through a large spray of water. They roared through the doorway to the starting platform and whooshed to a stop with a squeal of airbrakes.

"Oh my. Wow. That was fun." Josie laughed and wiped water from her arms. She glanced over at Sailor's too-pale face. "Sweetheart, are you okay?"

"I'm fine." Sailor reached a shaky arm toward the metal bar that held them in place and pushed it away. She stepped from the car and stumbled when she tried to take a step.

Josie caught up to her and took her arm. "That last segment was a bit topsy-turvy. I wasn't quite expecting it."

"Me either. I thought it would be more gentle hills and slow turns. From the outside it didn't look like it would be as violent as the other roller coasters we've seen."

"I agree. So, is that out of your system, or do we need to ride some other rides before settling in at the shows?"

"I think I'm good for now. An air-conditioned show sounds fine."

Mandy and Allie saw them coming and rose slowly to their feet.

"Ready for some air-conditioning?" Josie called out to them.

"More than ready. And a cold drink sounds good, too." Allie pointed to a drink stand.

They ordered lemonades and sipped on them as they headed down the pathway looking for something to do next. They discussed three show options before settling on a lively musical.

Sailor made a choking sound and hurried around the corner of a building. Josie motioned for Mandy and Allie to wait and followed. Sailor was leaning over a trash bin emptying her stomach.

"I knew we shouldn't have ridden that ride. Now you're going to be miserable all afternoon."

"No more miserable than I already felt."

Josie wondered if Sailor had pushed herself to ride because Brian was upset she didn't like the fast rides. That would explain why they weren't sitting together. "Look, I know you and Brian are on the outs, and I understand how frustrating that is, but making yourself sick isn't going to help."

"Riding the roller coaster was a choice I made for me. It has nothing to do with Brian."

"But why would you want to do something that would make you miserable?"

"I'll be fine after we sit for a while. That lemonade on the heels of the ride was obviously a bad idea. By the end of the show I'm sure I'll feel better. And if it makes *you* feel better, I promise not to ride anything else like that today."

"Fair enough. If you think you're up to it, let's get back to the girls. I'm sure they're worried about you."

Mandy studied Sailor with concerned eyes, but she didn't say anything. Josie was grateful for her intuition. They headed over to the theater and settled in.

TWELVE

"Josie, don't get mad at me for saying this," Mandy said, "but if I didn't know better, I'd say Sailor was pregnant."

Josie froze at the door to their hotel room, floored by Mandy's assertion. The others were downstairs eating pizza poolside, but Mandy had asked to go back to the room to settle in and relax. Her feet were swollen from the long day, and Cam suggested she put her feet up.

"Mandy, why would you say that?"

Mandy hesitated, staring with troubled eyes at the plate of pizza and the bottle of water she clutched in her hands. "It's just a hunch. I mean, I don't know — she just seems so angry and has for the past couple of days. She and Brian aren't talkin'. She isn't talkin' to me. She asked all those questions about what would happen if I rode the roller coaster, and suddenly she wants to ride one. She didn't want to ride anythin' like that yesterday."

"Anyone else but Sailor, and I'd say you might have something."

"I know. That's why I said, 'If I didn't know better.' But her actions remind me of myself when I found out I was expectin'."

"It's more likely that she was lashing out because of her fight with Brian. She was upset and wanted to do something daring and out of character for her."

"I sure hope so."

"So do I."

Josie opened the door and ushered Mandy inside. She waited while Mandy changed into comfortable clothes and found something to watch on TV. Once Josie had Mandy settled, she headed back down to join the others.

Josie chose to sit alone on the far side of the pool when she returned to the swim area. She wanted a few moments of quiet. She couldn't get Mandy's words out of her head. She kept playing them over and over while studying Sailor's actions as the evening wore on. She looked for a sign that would put her mind at ease, but instead she thought of all the times Sailor had been tired or queasy of late.

"A penny for your thoughts." Caleb startled her when he appeared at her side.

His eyes twinkled as he spun one of the plastic poolside chairs around backward and straddled it. "You look far too serious for a night like this."

It was a perfect evening to be outdoors. The air had cooled just enough to make their poolside seats comfortable. Matt and Seth had joined the kids in the water, but now they sat on the side of the pool talking. Brit, Allie, and Cameron rested on chairs behind them. A gentle breeze stirred the night air. Storm clouds gathered on the horizon, but for now the sky above them was clear.

In the water the kids stacked double for a multiplayer game of chicken. Josie sighed with relief when Brian ducked under the water and Sailor climbed onto his shoulders. He stood easily under her weight, and they fought it out with two of the middle-school boys. Squeals and laughter carried their way on the breeze.

"A penny isn't nearly enough to convince me to share my thoughts." Josie knew Caleb couldn't begin to pay her enough to share the scary thoughts she'd been having about Sailor.

"Ohh — must be something good running around in that head of yours." He leaned forward on the round plastic table, his fingertips almost touching hers. "C'mon, tell me."

"Never." A small thrill ran through her at his nearness. She changed the subject. "You seem to be in a much better mood tonight."

"I am." He glanced over his shoulder. "This teen drama stuff wears me out. It's different when it's one of the other kids in the youth group. I can be objective. But when it comes to Sailor" — he sighed — "it isn't nearly as easy. For now, though, it looks like another crisis has been averted. I'm free to enjoy my evening."

Josie smiled in agreement. "Yep. Whatever they were fighting about — they must have worked it out."

"Looks like it."

Caleb stared at her. His lips curled into a smile.

She squirmed under his gaze. "What?"

"Matt, Brit, Seth, and Cameron sent me over. They have an agenda."

Josie looked over at their friends. They each grinned and waved — their expressions were guilty.

"You came all the way over here because they sent you, not because you wanted to join me?" Her heart sank, but she tried not to let him see how much the thought upset her.

"Oh, I wanted to join you all right." His grin made her smile. "I was already on my way over when they stopped me."

"That's better. So what's their agenda?"

"They said we had the rough groups today, so they want us to go get ice cream. Alone. Just the two of us."

"Just like that?" She raised a suspicious eyebrow. "I actually thought we had the easy groups."

"Don't tell them that!" He leaned forward, his manner conspiratorial. "Besides, *you* might have had an easy group. I didn't. I had the middle-school boys, remember? But you didn't get to ride many rides, did you? That's kind of a bummer. So we're even."

"Middle-school boys. Enough said." She shuddered. "So what's the deal? They look guilty. There has to be a catch."

"We get to go alone, as long as we bring something back for them. I think they're all too tired and lazy to go get their own."

"So we're the gophers." She stood and tugged his hand. "Sounds good to me! What are we waiting for? Let's get out of here before we turn to pumpkins or worse — the kids get wind of what we're up to."

Caleb opened the gate and waited for her to pass through. "I don't know if you noticed, but I think there's a little matchmaking involved, too."

"We don't want to let them down, do we?" Josie would have to thank them later.

Caleb sent the foursome a thumbs-up sign and followed her out into the dimly lit parking lot. She stepped across the curb and stumbled on a broken piece of asphalt. Caleb was quick to right her. He tucked her hand protectively into the crook of his arm and slowed his pace. Her arm felt so right in his that she wouldn't have cared if they'd stopped walking completely.

The ice-cream stand was near the street next door. Several families and couples waited patiently in line. A spotlight shone down on the patrons, its light bright after the dark parking lot they'd just crossed, but several empty tables waited in the dim outskirts of the large patio. When it was their turn to order, Caleb asked for two soft-serve vanilla cones dipped in chocolate. They walked to one of the isolated tables on the outer circumference of the area to eat.

Ice cream already dripped from the rim of the cones. Caleb licked his. "Better eat fast. This humidity's making it melt faster than it usually would on such a nice evening."

She licked around the cone, trying to keep up with the melting. "How are we going to get their cones back to them?"

"I think we'll have to renege on our assignment, and they'll have to come over to eat in shifts. There's no way the ice cream will make it that far without us wearing it." He slurped his melting cone with a laugh. "In the meantime, we'll take full advantage of the quiet over here and eat as slowly as the melting ice cream will allow."

Unfortunately the ice cream melted in record time. The storm moved closer. Thunder rumbled in the distance.

"We'd better get back and send them over here, or they won't get their turn before the storm hits," Caleb said with great reluctance. He stood and helped Josie to her feet.

Josie licked the last remnants of the sweet cream from her lips. The moon came out from behind some clouds and illuminated the parking lot. "I ate so fast my lips are numb."

"I think I can help with that." Caleb's blue eyes grew soft, and he leaned in and surprised her with a gentle kiss. His lips were warm against hers. "How's that?"

"Much better. Thanks." Her words came out in a breathless whirl.

His voice had been strong and steady. How did he do it? The world had just tilted on its axis, but he didn't seem to notice.

Another rumble of thunder sounded to the west.

"Um, I guess we'd better get going." She wanted to stay. She wanted him to kiss her again.

"Yeah, I guess so," Caleb said. "I owe the others a debt of gratitude for sending me off with you. But if it wasn't thundering, I'd be fine with staying here a whole lot longer."

Josie grinned. "So would I."

The storm hit with a vengeance later that night, and Mandy, for all her independent bravado, asked if she could sleep with Josie. Allie and Sailor fell into the other bed, exhausted.

Josie remembered the night they'd found Mandy in the covered bridge a couple of weeks earlier and thanked God they were able to get to the lonely girl that evening before she had to ride out the scary storm alone.

The electricity had blinked off and on a few times as the storm passed overhead, pitching the room into darkness as they tried to get ready for bed. Though the red light from the alarm clock now lent the room a glow of light, Mandy lay frozen in place beside her on the bed. She'd seemed like a normal teen all day — albeit a teen with a seven-month-pregnant belly — but when she let her guard down due to the storm, she showed her fragility.

"Have you always disliked storms?" Josie asked quietly. She hoped if she kept Mandy talking, she'd get her mind off her fears.

"I didn't used to mind them, but I've had some bad experiences lately between Gina's boyfriend putting me outside in a few of them and then the night at the covered bridge. I've seen bolts of lightning actually hit nearby trees during some of the storms when Frank locked me out of the house."

"What an awful thing to do! Why would he do that?"

"He didn't want me there from the start. He found out I didn't like thunder, and that was that. It isn't the most relaxed feeling to be standing outside when something like that's going on."

"I can understand," Josie said. "But we're safe here. You know that, right?"

"I do. But I know the power these storms can have. The Joplin storm wasn't too far away from here."

"So you're afraid of tornadoes?"

"Tornadoes, lightning, flash floods, the dark. I'm sort of afraid of all of it now."

Josie prayed for the right words to say to her. "I recently faced a fear of my own.

Sailor and her dad helped me overcome it."

Mandy rolled onto her side and placed her head on her arm. "What were you afraid of? I can't imagine anything that would scare you."

"My aunt drowned in a lake when I was a child. My mother instilled the fear of water in us from that time on so none of us kids would go near a pool, pond, or lake. It worked."

"I'm sorry."

"Thanks." Josie smiled in the dark. Mandy had so many issues to deal with, but she was showing sympathy for Josie's bad experience — another positive sign that the teen would be able to overcome her circumstances.

"So how did they help you face your fears?"

"They took me out on a boat and realized how bad my fear of the water was. Caleb said I couldn't live like that, that there's too much water in the area since we live on a lake. He immediately got me in the water over at the public pool — the shallow water where I could touch bottom and feel safe. We started with the basics, and before I knew it, I was feeling more confident."

"How would I work through my fears? Do I have to go out and stand in another storm?

Challenge it?" Her voice shook.

"Goodness, no." Josie laughed quietly. "I'd never ask you to do something like that. But you're making a good start right now by sharing your fears with me. Talking about them is another step in getting past the fear."

"And after that?"

"You could walk over to the window with me, and we could watch the storm from a safe place. Sometimes that helps, too."

"As long as you go with me."

"I will." Josie slipped from the bed and used her cell phone to light the way. The last thing she needed was for Mandy to trip and fall. They stepped to the window and slipped behind the curtain.

Sailor and Allie continued to sleep soundly in the darkened room.

Josie and Mandy's window looked over the hotel complex next door. A color-changing pool light lit the empty in-ground pool that had been filled with vacationers a couple of hours earlier. A trio of girls ran up the covered walkway to watch the storm from the building's balcony.

"They're crazy." Mandy laughed.

"I think so, too," Josie said. "I don't mind storms quite as much as you do, but I sure wouldn't be out there running around in one. I prefer the dry warmth of our room, thank you very much."

"Me, too." Mandy sidled against Josie as they watched the rain pound the pavement during flashes of lightning. "It's kind of beautiful from here."

"I agree. There's something about feeling safe that makes it easier to face a fear. I'd find it hard to be brave while outdoors in the elements. You had every reason to be scared."

"So I'm safe inside a sturdy building right now, but what about our building in Lullaby? Is it safe? Will the lake ever flood enough to come up to our building? You were scared of water — did you worry that the lake would rise in a storm? How do I let go of my fears so we can both get to sleep?"

"Wow, you're on a roll. Yes, our building is safe. It's very safe. Those buildings have withstood far harsher storms than this one. The lake won't ever flood our building. There's a dam at the far end, and they can let water out if they feel flooding will be an issue. I've truly faced my fear about the water, and I feel I can swim well enough to keep me safe no matter what the water will bring." Josie let the curtain drop in place and again used her phone for its dim light. "Now let's go back to bed, and I'll pray."

They lay down, and Josie prayed for Mandy's peace of mind, and that her fear would be lifted from her. She also prayed that Mandy would find forgiveness for Gina and Gina's boyfriend, Frank. Mandy lay silent, but Josie could tell she listened to the prayer.

Mandy whispered a heartfelt "Amen" as Josie finished. "Why did you bring up Gina?"

"Because sometimes we hold on to bitterness and anger, and it can affect our relationship with God. That can fuel the fire of our fears. By letting go of those issues, we open ourselves up for a better relationship with our Savior, and we allow Him to work in us. You don't want anything to be a stumbling block in your relationship with Him."

"I agree." Mandy yawned.

"Trust goes a long way in bringing peace. Trust in Him, and that He'll watch over you and keep you safe, and I think you'll find peace even in life's harshest storms."

"Thanks, Josie."

The storm quieted, and Mandy's breathing became steady. Josie fell asleep thanking God for His protection and for Mandy's peace of mind.

THIRTEEN

Caleb poked his head out from the back room as Josie entered the shop late in the afternoon on their first day back after their Branson trip. "I have an errand for you to run. Do you mind?"

"Not at all. Where do you need me to go?"

"We're out of several basic supplies, and my order won't be in for a few more days. The candy shop over in Dixie put a box together for us. I just need you to pick it up. We'll replace it after we get our inventory."

"I can do that. Let me grab my purse and my car keys from my suite, and I'll head over there." She stopped with a hand on the doorknob. "Do you want me to send Mandy over to help you out? She loves working here."

"I'd love that. I know she wants to learn more about the business, and Sailor's been gone all afternoon."

"Okay. Mandy will be here in a few, and I'll be back in a couple of hours."

Josie loved the scenery on the drive to Dixie. Mandy had been more than happy to fill some hours at the candy shop — she'd already asked if she could work part time there, which worked out great since Josie was spending more time at the pregnancy center as it grew busier.

She arrived at the other candy shop in record time, stowed the box in her car, and debated grabbing a bite to eat at the cute little diner across the street. It was well past dinner time, but she thought better of it since Caleb had seemed in a hurry to get the box of goodies from his friend.

The quaint buildings that made up the town hugged the side of the mountain. Josie drove slowly past the colorful Victorian storefronts, window shopping from her car. The tourists were heading home with back-to-school responsibilities pressing in on them. Josie relished the chance to see the town without tons of cars making the journey a challenge.

A familiar motorcycle parked in front of a cheery yellow building caught her eye. Brian sat on the bike with his helmet in his hands. He stared off into space, looking dejected.

Josie pulled in beside him and rolled down

her window. "Hey, Brian, is everything okay?"

Brian startled then looked at the building in panic. Josie followed his gaze. Her heart sank as she registered what the building represented. She turned off the car, opened the car door, and was at his side in two steps. "Brian. This is an abortion clinic. Is Sailor in there?"

He barely nodded, not looking her in the eye.

"How long, Brian? How long has Sailor been in there?" Josie felt sick to her stomach.

"I don't know." His voice sounded anguished. "I'm so sorry. She's been in there awhile."

"And you didn't have the decency to at least accompany her inside?" She'd never felt so angry at a person. Josie turned and took the steps two at a time. She heard the motorcycle start up as she entered the door to the clinic. Good riddance. She didn't have time to worry about Brian.

A receptionist opened a glass window. "May I help you?"

"Yes." Josie tried to catch her breath. Her accent thickened in times of stress. "I need to speak to Sailor Jackson. Now."

"I'm sorry, ma'am. As I'm sure you'll understand, our clients expect the utmost confidentiality. I can't give out any information on who is or isn't here."

"I know she's here, and I want to speak to her now."

"Ma'am — I'm going to have to ask you to leave. If you don't, I'll be forced to call the authorities."

"Call whoever you want." Josie headed for the inner door. *"Sailor!"*

The receptionist picked up her phone and started tapping numbers.

Josie kept walking.

A door to her left opened, and Sailor walked out. She looked awful.

"Oh, Sailor."

Sailor spun around and burst into tears. She looked young and frail. Her hair was a tangled mess. Josie had never seen her look so wan. A nurse with a ferocious scowl followed her out the door and into the waiting area.

"You need to come back in here right now. We aren't finished with you."

"Oh yes you are." Josie stepped between the woman and Sailor.

Sailor's hiccupping sobs filled the room.

Josie stepped backward and clasped Sailor's arm with one hand. She wanted to make sure no one grabbed her from another direction and hauled her off into the depths of the clinic. She continued to push Sailor toward the door.

"We're leaving, and you'd all be advised to keep your distance and stay away from us."

Sailor clutched Josie's arm like a lifeline.

Josie gripped the knob to the outer door and pulled it open. A burst of fresh air filled her lungs as she finally remembered to breathe. "Let's get out of here."

They hurried down the cold stone steps to the car, where Josie settled Sailor in the passenger seat. She hurried around to her own side and slid inside before pushing the button to lock the doors. The locks snapped down with a reassuring sound. She buckled her seatbelt and tried to shake the creepy feeling the clinic had brought on. She'd never in her life felt such a dark, oppressive atmosphere as she had inside that building. The entire town had taken on a nightmarish quality. Tears rolled down her face as she turned to study Sailor. "Are you okay?"

"N–no." Sailor shook her head and sobbed into her hands. "I don't th–think I'll ever be o–okay again."

Josie felt the teen was on the edge of hysteria. The clinic's door opened, and the hateful nurse stood in the entry staring at them. Josie reached over and clicked Sailor's seatbelt into place then threw the car into gear and drove away from the building as fast as she could. She headed for a small roadside park she'd noticed on the way into town.

"Do you need medical attention?" she asked. She hoped not. The nearest hospital, the only one she knew of, was on the far side of Lullaby.

Sailor's sobs had stopped, but she seemed to have withdrawn inside herself. She shook her head no.

Josie pulled into a deserted parking spot and turned off the ignition. "Tell me what happened."

"Brian left me."

"He was waiting outside when I drove up. He looked distraught. I asked where you were, and he panicked."

"Wonderful." Sailor hiccupped. "The jerk."

"Sailor." Josie tried to wrap her mind around the fact that she'd just pulled her from such a place. "An abortion clinic? Why would you feel you had to go to a place like that? Why didn't you confide in me, or Cameron, or your dad?"

"My dad will hate me when he finds out about this. I didn't want him to know." Sailor's voice cracked as another round of tears started. "And I knew you and Cameron would tell him if I went to either of you."

"First of all, your dad could never hate you." Josie pushed Sailor's hair away from her face. "Second of all, Sailor, we're all here for you. We love you. Why would you ever feel you had to go to such extremes?"

"It was Brian's idea. He said it would make it all go away. My dad wouldn't hate him. He wouldn't hate me. He'd never have to know."

"Oh, baby."

Sailor flung off the seatbelt and threw herself into Josie's arms. Josie held her.

"That's why Brian wouldn't speak to me at the amusement park." She sobbed against Josie's shoulder. "I wouldn't agree to *take care* of it."

"And it's why you wanted to ride the roller coaster."

"Yes. But all I did was throw up. I was so scared. I didn't want Brian mad at me — he's the only person I could talk to about this, so I agreed to come here with him." Fresh tears poured from her eyes. "We were only together once, Josie. I didn't think one time would matter."

"It only takes one time, Sailor." Josie thought for a moment. "Look. I need to get you back to the clinic. I want Cameron to check you. She might recommend we go to the hospital."

Sailor's voice rose to a high pitch. "No, Josie! I'm fine. I don't want to go to the hospital. I just want to go home."

"But you don't know what they did. I'm out of my league in this area. The nurse said you weren't finished and needed to go back in."

"They weren't finished because I never gave them a chance to start. I felt the worst feeling ever when I walked into that building. It got worse with every single step. When I got called back to the examination room, I felt like I couldn't breathe. I knew I had to get out of there. The nurse stepped out of the room so I could change into a gown, and I flew out of there as fast as I could go. I've never been as happy in my life to see anyone as I was to see you standing on the other side of that door. I was so scared they'd grab me and drag me back in. And from the look on that nurse's face after she chased us outside, that's exactly what she would have done."

Sailor didn't stop shaking. Josie was afraid she was going into shock. She reached over the seat and pulled the beach towel from her swimming bag. She wrapped it around

224

Sailor and held her tight. "It's okay. You're safe now."

"I have to tell my dad, don't I?"

"Yes, but I'll tell him with you. Or if you want me to, I'll talk to him first. I think I can help soften the blow."

Josie took Sailor up the back stairs to Caleb's loft and helped her settle into bed. "Try to get some rest. I'll be back soon. I'm going to talk to your dad. He needs to know what's going on. You need closure on this. I'm calling Cameron to come over and stay with you." She dialed Cameron at the clinic as she walked from the room. She explained the situation, and Cameron immediately headed over. As soon as Josie knew Sailor had someone watching over her, she went to the shop.

She walked to the car to get the box of supplies before returning to the back entrance. She stepped into the hall of the shop. She could hear Caleb shuffling papers in his office. She placed the box on a nearby counter and rested her elbows on it. She lowered her bowed head to her hands.

Lord, thank You for bringing Sailor and her baby safely through this stage of the journey. I ask, Lord, that You give her the strength she'll need in order to live with the repercus-

sions of her choices. Please give me the proper words to say to Caleb when I talk to him about this, and let him have the right heart to hear them. I ask in Your name that You can help him find peace over this so he can be the supportive father Sailor needs. In Your name, Amen.

She stepped around the corner to stand in his open doorway.

"Hey, you're back!" His face lit up when he saw her. "I'm glad."

You won't be when you hear what I have to say.

He looked down at the mess on his desk. "Give me a second to tidy up this paperwork, and I'll help you unload the package. Did the trip go okay? Did you find the other shop without a problem?"

Josie dropped her chin to her chest and closed her eyes for a moment. She opened them again. She ignored his first question. "I found the shop easily enough. I just got back a little bit ago. Um, is Mandy doing okay with running the front?"

"Yes. She's doing a great job." Caleb glanced up at Josie, and his smile faltered. "What is it? What's wrong?"

Josie hated to be the one to ruin his day, but Sailor was too upset to be the one to start this conversation.

"Caleb, I need to talk to you. In private. Can we talk here in your office?"

His forehead furrowed. "Sure. Let me tell Mandy to give us a few minutes."

Josie nodded and stepped aside to let him pass.

He stopped next to her in the doorway and caressed her cheek. "Are you okay?"

She nodded. "Yes. This isn't about me."

"Okay." Relief flooded his features. "Good. I'll be right back."

She dropped into a seat opposite his desk. She hated knowing that the next few minutes of their conversation would forever change his world.

He looked somber when he reentered the room. He closed the door and sat in the chair next to her.

Josie had trouble meeting his eyes. Her own eyes filled with tears. She tried to blink them back.

"What is it? You're scaring me."

"I saw . . . one of the girls from the youth group when I was over in Dixie." Her vision blurred. She so didn't want to be the one to tell him this.

"Okay." His expression was masked in confusion. "Did something happen to this girl?"

"Something had already happened, yes."

227

She reached out to touch his hand then drew back before she could connect.

"Tell me." He reached over and clasped her hand in his. "Whatever it is, we'll get through it together."

"Caleb — she was at the abortion clinic over there." Her voice broke. She could hardly stand the look of compassion on his face. The way she'd phrased it, of course he'd assume it was anyone but Sailor.

His face clouded with pain. "Then we've failed her. We have all this support with the pregnancy center, but we've let one of our own fall through the cracks. I've tried to tell the kids they can come to any one of us with anything, and we'll help them through it. Why didn't she come to us? Did you talk to her? Is she okay?"

"She didn't follow through, Caleb. We didn't fail her. But she was so terrified to tell the people she loved, that she almost did the unthinkable. She said she didn't want them to hate her."

Caleb was on his feet, tugging at her hand, trying to get her to stand. "Then we need to go to her right now and help her tell her family. This isn't something she should do alone. She's apparently carried this burden alone for far too long. I'll drive, and you call whoever it is and let her know we're coming."

Josie remained in her seat. "Caleb. Wait."

"What?" He lowered himself into his chair. "We need to go to her, Josie. The sooner the better."

"I know we do, but for now she's safe, and she has someone with her. I need to ask you something. Remember the other day when you said that you could stay objective, as long as you were dealing with one of your youth group members?"

He nodded. "Yes. That's why I want to go to her. I can't imagine what I'd do if it were Sailor, but I hope I'd be rational. I wouldn't want to be blindsided, though. I'd want someone who cares to give me a heads up. We need to diffuse the situation with this girl, because her family's reaction is going to have everything to do with how she moves forward with this."

"I agree. This young girl needs support, not judgment or anger. She doesn't need to see disappointment in the eyes of those who love her. Not right now. Not ever." She stared at him, reading the confusion in his eyes. She silently pleaded with him to understand. She willed him not to make her say it out loud.

He looked down at their clasped hands. He absently rubbed his thumb against hers, caressing her, even as he tried to make sense of what she wasn't telling him.

"Caleb." Her voice cracked, and she whispered, "I'm giving you that heads up."

Her tears fell freely.

"No." Realization transformed his features. "Sailor?" he asked. Horror laced the single word. "*Sailor* was at the abortion clinic?"

She nodded.

He dropped her hand and walked stiffly around his desk. He stopped by his file cabinet and stared at a framed photo that showed a smiling, gap-toothed Sailor — she couldn't have been more than six years old when it was taken.

He kept his back to her. "Where is she now?"

"Upstairs. I had her lay down. She's exhausted. Cameron's with her."

"How could you not tell me?" His voice was hoarse with emotion.

"I just did."

"No — why didn't you call me the minute you found her there?"

Stunned, Josie made her way to her feet. "She was falling apart, Caleb. I had to calm her down."

"But you didn't call me after that."

"This isn't the type of thing you can tell

someone over the phone. I prayed and handled it in the way I felt was best. Do you think it would be better if Sailor were here to see this reaction from you? This is why I told you the way I did. So you'd at least try to be objective with her like you would be for any of the other girls in the youth group."

"Josie." He spun on her with eyes filled with fury. "Dixie is over *thirty minutes* away from here. Why didn't you call me after you calmed her down? Did you know about her pregnancy before today? Did you know that Sailor was expecting? Who else knows about this?"

Josie stepped backward. She hadn't expected this anger. She especially hadn't expected his anger to be directed at her. "I didn't know about any of it. You sent me to Dixie, remember? I happened upon her, and when I did, I did what I felt best at the time."

"She's not your daughter, Josie. You had no right to keep this from me. You should have told me straight up. I think you'd better leave."

"Don't you think it'd be better if I —"

"No. Just. Go." He turned his back on her. His posture was rigid with anger.

Josie felt a shot of anger herself. "Look,

Caleb, whether you like it or not — whether you are angry at the world or whatever — Sailor needs your support. I'll leave, but I hope you'll take my words and intentions to heart before you go storming up there and ruin the only other female relationship you have."

She turned on her heel and hurried out the back door. The sobs overtook her before she cleared the back deck. The deck where they'd had meals together. The deck where they'd built their friendship. The deck where she'd let herself hope their friendship would grow to something more.

She didn't mind that he'd lashed out at her. She'd expected it. People tended to shoot the messenger when they were angry or upset after hearing bad news. In fact, she'd hoped he'd unload on her, and then he'd be ready to face Sailor with love and compassion. But she hadn't expected to have such raw anger directed at her, unleashed in fury by the man she loved.

FOURTEEN

Caleb sank down in his desk chair. He felt like he couldn't catch his breath. He knew he was wrong to lash out at Josie, but it was too late now to focus on that. Sailor was upstairs hurting, and she'd barely escaped making a bad situation worse by considering abortion. That's what had caused his anger. He couldn't believe she'd thought even for a minute that he'd rather see her end her pregnancy than to *disappoint* him.

Josie had felt bad when she thought Mandy had felt her judgment. How much worse was this? How could his own daughter feel that his love was so conditional? He had his work cut out for him. He had to mend his relationship with her.

He didn't know how to face Sailor without breaking down. She'd see his anguish no matter how he tried to mask it. He'd tried so hard to instill trust in his youth group, in Josie, and yet he'd failed to build that same relationship with the most important person in his life.

One thing he did know, Sailor needed him now, and he was going to her. He walked out into the prep room and splashed cold water on his face. Mandy popped her head around the corner. "I thought I heard you back here. No one's come by in the past hour. Do you want me to shut'er down?"

"Yes. Thanks, Mandy." He dried his face and hands. "Do you need my help with anything?"

He couldn't believe how calm he sounded on the heels of such a revelation.

"No. I don't need any help. I remember everything you showed me." Concern scrunched her features. "You don't look so good. What's wrong?"

"I need to go upstairs to Sailor. She isn't feeling well. Can you lock up before you head out?"

"Sure."

"Thanks."

"Caleb?"

"Yeah?"

"Is there anything I can do to help?"

"Just pray for us. And if you don't mind, tell Josie I'm sorry."

"You're sorry for what?"

"She'll know what I mean."

"Okay. Whatever is goin' on, I'll be prayin' for you."

Caleb nodded and left the shop in her hands. He trudged upstairs, knowing his own daughter probably cringed at every footfall, dreading his arrival in their living quarters. Would she feign sleep? Would she hide under the covers? Would she stare at him with the same look of anger that Josie had worn when lashing back at him? *I hope you'll take my words and intentions to heart before you go storming up there and ruin the only other female relationship you have.*

In one broken moment, he'd botched everything. Josie was only trying to help, trying to make it as smooth as possible on all of them. Yet he'd hurt her deeply by reacting as he had. He didn't know if he'd damaged their future forever — time would tell on that issue — but for now, he could honor her courage by doing the right thing for Sailor.

Sailor's door was open, the room dim.

Cameron sat on the edge of Sailor's bed. "She's sleeping. She's had a rough time of it."

He stood in the doorway and studied his sleeping daughter. She looked so young. He motioned Cameron out of the room.

She followed and pulled the door shut

behind her.

"How is she?"

"Physically, she's fine. I listened to the baby's heartbeat, and it's strong. Even with all the turmoil, both baby and momma are doing well."

Momma. His seventeen-year-old daughter. "Physically, she's fine — but emotionally?"

"She's emotionally drained and scared to death of your reaction. She's further along than I'd have imagined. She's already into her second trimester."

"Can you put that in English for me?"

"The baby will be due sometime in January. She's well into her fourth month. She'll be showing soon."

He sank onto the couch.

Cameron sat down beside him. "How are you doing?"

"Let's see. I just found out my teenage daughter is pregnant. I lashed out in a totally unacceptable way at the woman I love — when all she tried to do was help me. And I feel like a failure as both a youth leader and a pastor." He ticked each item off with a finger as he mentioned it.

"Sounds like a perfectly normal reaction to me on all counts." She reached out to pat his arm. "But on the flip side, you're now calm and ready to go in and face your

236

daughter with love and rationality. You've proven to your youth group and their parents that you're human. This will help you be a better leader once you walk a bit farther on this new path. And as for Josie — I assume you're talking about her when you talk about the woman you love — she'll forgive you. I promise she'll understand."

"I messed things up royally tonight."

"Understandably."

"Daddy?" Sailor's quiet voice drifted to him from the direction of her bedroom.

He hurried to her side. For a moment she stood frozen in the doorway. Then with a burst of long-forgotten little-girl abandon, she threw herself into the safety of his arms. "Oh, Daddy, I'm so sorry."

Tears of compassion coursed down his cheeks. "It's okay, baby. We're going to get through this. We'll get through it together, just like we've gotten through everything else."

She clung to him. "You don't hate me?"

"I could never hate you. You should know that by now."

"I know I'm a disappointment. I'm going to cause you problems with your career. People are going to talk."

"You'll never be a disappointment, Sailor. Look at me." He tipped her chin so she had to look up at him. "Nothing you can do can ever change my love for you. I'm disappointed that your life will be harder than it has to be. I only want the best for you. People will talk no matter what. You're far more important than my career, but as Cameron said, it'll give us another facet in being able to relate and have compassion for other families going through hard times. Most importantly, God will use this for His greater good — you just wait and see."

The doorbell rang.

Caleb glanced over at Cameron.

"I bet that's Josie. You all carry on, and I'll go down and let her in."

Caleb led Sailor over to the sofa. She snuggled against his side. If nothing else, the huge wall that had recently stood between them had crumbled.

Slow footfalls announced the arrival of a guest. Josie's footsteps were bouncy and quick, even when she was upset.

Brian rounded the corner and stepped into the room.

"You." Caleb reared to his feet. The vein in his temple throbbed. "You have some nerve coming here tonight."

"I do, sir. I came to right a wrong."

"You can't right this wrong."

Cameron slipped around Brian and

wrapped her arm around him. "Why don't we all sit down?"

"I came to stand up to you like a man," Brian said. "First of all, Sailor" — he turned to her — "I'm so sorry for taking off like I did today. When Josie drove up, I panicked. I knew she'd take good care of you."

Sailor's only reaction was a shrug.

Brian choked up. "I'm sorry, to both of you, for everything. Sailor, I don't know if you'll ever forgive me for what I put you through, but I was wrong. I should never have asked you to get an abortion." He stood. "I hope you'll someday find it in your heart to forgive me."

Caleb wanted to let him suffer, but he knew he couldn't. "Sit down, boy. She didn't go through with the procedure."

Hope flickered in Brian's eyes. Maybe the kid wasn't so bad after all. If he'd really wanted her to follow through, he would have had a different emotion upon hearing that she'd changed her mind — disappointment or maybe even anger.

"I'm such an idiot. Josie stopped you in time?" His knees buckled, and he sank onto the easy chair. "Thank you, Lord."

"Josie didn't stop me. I made the decision on my own. But if I hadn't, Josie would have torn the doors off the hinges trying to stop me. Trust me. You should have seen her. She was so angry when she took on the receptionist and the nurse."

"She took on the receptionist and the nurse?" Caleb grinned for the first time that evening.

"Yeah, she did. The receptionist was threatening to call the authorities, and Josie told her to go for it. I heard her through the door. She was *mad.*"

"Good for her."

Sailor looked at him with a raised eyebrow. "What?"

"Seems to me," Sailor said, "you have some explaining to do to a certain someone who isn't in this room."

"Now?"

"There's no time better. If you love her, you need to go tell her. She was *there* for me, Dad. If you bawled her out for that, you need to make things right."

"Cameron? Can you stay a bit longer and chaperone? It seems I have an apology to make."

"I can stay as long as you need me."

Caleb made a quick trip to his downstairs office to grab something out of his desk drawer before heading over to see Josie.

He knocked on the outer door of the

pregnancy center, waited a few moments, then resorted to using the bell. He even called up to her balcony doors. "Josie! It's me. Open up. I need to speak with you."

The downstairs door finally opened, but Mandy was the one who answered. "She isn't home."

"But it's dark out. Where could she have gone?"

"I don't know, but she isn't here."

"Okay. I'm sorry I bothered you. We'll explain everything later. If she comes home will you have her call me? No matter how late it is."

"I doubt she'll be all that late. We're talking Josie here. She's totally responsible, and it's a work night."

"Yeah, well, even the most responsible of people can do strange things when they're upset."

"You upset Josie? What did you do to her?" Mandy's back was up.

"Nothing I can't fix. I hope. Just — have her call me, please?"

Mandy narrowed her eyes. "I'll give her the message, but it'll be up to her whether or not she wants to talk to you."

"Fair enough. Thanks, Mandy."

He walked away smiling. Mandy was going to be fine. She wasn't going to kiss up

241

to him just to keep a job. If he hurt Josie, and Josie didn't want to forgive him? Mandy would feel the same way. Her ability to attach so strongly to Josie was a healthy sign.

The water called to him. He wasn't ready to go back to the house. He knew Cameron had things under control with the kids, and he figured he'd just be in the way. They needed to talk and work through things without Sailor's hot-headed dad in the room distracting them. He headed for the dock. He'd watch for Josie from there, and maybe he could intercept her before Mandy got involved.

The L-shaped dock went out into the water for about fifty feet before turning to the right to form the short leg. A noise carried over the water from the far end. Caleb slowed his steps. The last thing he needed was an altercation with someone tampering with his boats.

"Who's out there?"

His answer was silence. With quiet steps, he rounded the corner of the dock.

A lone woman sat at the end with her feet dangling in the water.

"Josie." He'd know that silhouette anywhere.

She froze but didn't respond.

"I know I've made a mess of things." He

walked the last few yards to join her. "I'm really sorry."

Her shoulders dropped just a bit.

"Can I join you?"

"It's your dock."

Her accent was thick, and her words were clipped. Not the answer he'd hoped to hear, but he'd grovel or apologize or sit in silence for as long as she wanted — as long as she forgave him in the end.

"I took your advice and calmed down before talking to Sailor. We're good."

Josie's eyes lit up in the moonlight. "She's doing okay? I'm so glad to hear that."

"Brian showed up. He's up there with her now."

"Alone?" Josie started to her feet.

Caleb held her in place with a hand to her shoulder. When he realized what he'd done, he quickly moved it away. "Cameron's up there with them. Brian seemed to have a change of heart. He was devastated at what he'd made her do, but when he found out she didn't go through with it, he cried with relief."

"So they're going to be okay?"

He sighed. "Yeah. I guess so."

Josie stared out at the water.

"I shouldn't have lashed out at you like that. It's inexcusable. Sailor told me what you did at the clinic. She said you were ready to take on the whole place if that's what it took to get her out of there."

She huffed a dry laugh. "Lucky for me she was already on her way out. I doubt I could have done much for all my bravado. They weren't nice people at all."

"No, they weren't. Anyone willing to hurt my grandbaby deserves whatever you planned to give them and then some."

"Your grandbaby?" For the first time Josie's stance softened.

"Yeah. My grandbaby. How do you like that? According to Cameron, we'll get a bonus Christmas present a month late."

"Congratulations, Grandpa."

He cringed. "Can we take it easy on that aspect? I'm not going to be there for another five months. Let me age with dignity."

This time her smile was genuine and solely for him. "I'm glad you calmed down before going up to her."

"Only because of the wise advice of a friend."

"A friend, huh? Do I know her?"

"You are her."

"Hmm. Well, when Cameron called me a few minutes ago, she said you used some choice words that had nothing to do with friendship."

He felt his face flush. Thank heavens for the cover of darkness. "She, uh, she called you, huh? What else did she have to say?"

"She was rambling. She wanted to talk to me before you did. But she said something about you proclaiming your undying love for me or something to that effect." She peered up at him, trying to see his expression in the moonlight. "Don't worry. I know how Cameron romanticizes things. I took what she said with a grain of salt."

She kicked the water with her bare foot.

"You shouldn't have."

"Shouldn't have what?" Puzzled, she turned her head toward him.

"You shouldn't have discounted what she said." He leaned in and brushed her lips with his. "I did say it. And I meant it."

Josie froze in place. "You said you loved me? In front of Sailor, Cameron, and Brian?"

"Yes."

He fumbled for the box he'd pulled from his desk. "I've been carrying this around, waiting for the right time to give it to you." He handed her the package.

She carefully opened it and pulled out a gleaming necklace. "My stone."

"Right. The stone you found at the beach that first time out on the water. I wanted you to have something so you could always remember the way you faced your fears. I polished the stone and had it mounted in a necklace for you. I hope you like it."

"I love it." She turned and lifted her hair so he could clasp it around her neck. He leaned in and pressed his lips against the delicate curve.

"Josie, I know we just met a little over a month ago. We haven't known each other very long, and I'm willing to follow your lead. But, Josie, I've learned that life is short, and sometimes if you wait too long for something, it'll be gone. I don't want to lose you."

"You aren't going to lose me, Caleb. I'm not going anywhere."

"This will probably sound crazy, but how do you feel about having a very full house? I mean, you said you'd dreamed of marrying and having a few babies, but we'd have to do things out of order. You have Mandy, and I have Sailor. Both girls are due to have babies in the next year. They'll need a lot of support and help."

"Are you asking me to hire on as your nanny, Caleb?" Josie's eyes twinkled with laughter.

"Oh gosh, no. I'm really making a mess of this, aren't I?" He ran a hand through his already-mussed hair. "I'm not asking you to become our nanny. I'm asking if you'd consider building a family with me — if you'll marry me and be my wife."

"I'd love to." She sealed the deal with a kiss.

"It'll be a lot to take on. I mean, they'll have to replace you at the center, at least as live-in staff. I'd like to check into adopting Mandy. I know she's older and all, but she belongs with us. That means in a short amount of time we'll marry, we'll become parents to two beautiful daughters, we'll have two babies in the house, and possibly more babies to come after that."

"More babies? For us or for Sailor?"

"Us of course."

"Are you already trying to talk me out of my decision to say yes, fiancé? Are you getting cold feet?"

"No," he whispered against her lips. "My feet are warmer than they've ever been."

She snuggled into his strong embrace, and together they watched as the moon rose over the water.

ABOUT THE AUTHOR

Paige Winship Dooly is the author of over a dozen books and novellas. She enjoys living in the coastal Deep South with her family, after having grown up in the sometimes extremely cold Midwest. She is happily married to her high school sweetheart and loves their life of adventure in a full house with six homeschooled children and two dogs.

The employees of Thorndike Press hope you have enjoyed this Large Print book. All our Thorndike, Wheeler, and Kennebec Large Print titles are designed for easy reading, and all our books are made to last. Other Thorndike Press Large Print books are available at your library, through selected bookstores, or directly from us.

For information about titles, please call:
  (800) 223-1244

or visit our Web site at:
  http://gale.cengage.com/thorndike

To share your comments, please write:
  Publisher
  Thorndike Press
  10 Water St., Suite 310
  Waterville, ME 04901

7-2020-354   +